"You're v...
yourself, Mr. Ramsey."

"Confidence gets results, Dr. Barnes."

"Up until now, confidence might have gotten you results," she said sweetly.

"Are you suggesting I should change tactics?"

"I'm suggesting you abandon the project."

"I don't think so. You're an interesting challenge."

Marcia's nostrils flared. "Now you're being insulting."

Quentin stepped closer and said softly, "You liked it when I touched you."

Gritting her teeth, Marcia thought about icebergs and glaciers and Scotch on the rocks—anything to prevent herself from blushing. "You took me by surprise, that's all."

"You really get under my skin, Marcia Barnes."

"That's mutual." She had never been kissed like that in her life. Brief, beautiful and bewildering.

Dear Reader,

Welcome to the third of three scintillating books by Sandra Field. When Sandra first came up with the idea for her book *Beyond Reach* (#1806) she fell in love with her characters so much that she couldn't bear the thought of leaving them behind. So she wrote another book. Then another.... And *Significant Others* was born. Sandra writes:

"This series of three books crept up on me unawares. After Troy and Lucy met in the West Indies, I found myself curious to discover how marriage would change them, hence *Second Honeymoon* (#1830), again set on an island, this time off the coast of Nova Scotia. Lucy's laid-back friend, Quentin, and her uptight sister, Marcia, played minor roles in *Second Honeymoon*. Once Quentin had appeared on the scene, I knew I wouldn't rest until I'd brought him face-to-face with Marcia...."

After Hours is Marcia and Quentin's story.

Enjoy!

The Editor

SANDRA FIELD

After Hours

Harlequin Books

TORONTO • NEW YORK • LONDON
AMSTERDAM • PARIS • SYDNEY • HAMBURG
STOCKHOLM • ATHENS • TOKYO • MILAN
MADRID • WARSAW • BUDAPEST • AUCKLAND

ISBN 0-373-11862-7

AFTER HOURS

First North American Publication 1997.

CHAPTER ONE

SHE was losing it. Going bonkers.

Marcia Barnes stood in the living room of her condo, gazing out the window at the Rideau Canal; along the bicycle path that followed the curves of the canal a couple of intrepid cyclers zipped along, undeterred by the rain. It was a peaceful scene. Trees that had just burst into leaf, tulips in geometric beds, tidy arrays of well-kept houses. Everything neat and in perfect order.

Not like her.

She pulled a hideous face in the plate glass window. However, if this had been an attempt to quell the anxiety that had been with her ever since the meeting that afternoon at the medical research institute where she worked as an immunologist, it failed miserably. At the meeting the director, in a voice as smooth as cream, had spoken of budgetary restraints that might lead to cutbacks in staff. Cutbacks that could go as high as fifty percent. Although Marcia had worked there for seven years, she by no means had seniority.

Her work was her life. Had been as long as she could remember. She'd be lost without it.

She took a couple of deep breaths, trying to calm herself. Thank goodness she'd had the sense to refuse Lucy and Troy's invitation to dinner. Bad enough that she'd agreed to go to the gallery where their friend Quentin what's-his-name's show was opening.

Quentin. The name conjured up Harris tweed jackets and a pipe. An uppercrust British accent. Landscapes modeled after Constable's, with puffy white clouds and placid brown cows.

The last thing she felt right now was placid—she who everyone thought was so into control. Rather, she felt as though her life, so carefully constructed and so rigidly maintained, was falling into pieces around her.

She went into the kitchen and located her invitation to the gallery—the most exclusive gallery in town. Not that she cared. She didn't want to get dressed up and go out again. She didn't want to meet Quentin Ramsey, whose show, called *Multiple Personalities*, was being touted in such glowing terms. Nor did she want to see her sister Lucy and her brother-in-law Troy, who had arrived in Ottawa yesterday just to be at the opening.

What she wanted to do was fill her bathtub to the rim with steaming hot water and big globs of bubble bath, turn on the most soothing music she possessed and forget all about the outside world. After that she'd go to bed. How else to end a day from hell?

She sighed. Lucy was already puzzled by her refusal to have dinner with them. Although Lucy and Troy lived in Vancouver, they were spending the next two months in Ottawa because Troy was teaching pediatric residencies in two of the city hospitals. They'd brought the baby with them. If Marcia didn't turn up at the art gallery, Lucy would think something was wrong.

Nothing's wrong, Marcia thought wildly, rubbing at her forehead. There's a good chance I'm going to lose my job, the woman I've always been has deserted me and I don't have a clue who else to be, and I don't want to see my own sister. I don't even want to be around her. What kind of person does that make me?

Tall, beautiful Lucy, with her mop of untidy curls and her full figure and her rich, uninhibited laughter was the very antithesis of her elder sister Marcia. Or her younger sister Catherine. Or their mother Evelyn, come to that.

Do I envy her? Is that what it is?

Was envy one of the seven deadly sins? If it wasn't, it should be.

The old-fashioned grandfather clock, which had indeed belonged to Marcia's grandfather, a renowned neurosurgeon, chimed the half hour. I'm going to be late... Oh, well, that means I'll miss the speeches at the beginning and I'll get to meet Lucy and Troy in the middle of a whole lot of people. No chance for intimacy. Sounds good.

Marcia went into the bedroom, which faced west and was filled with the fading light of evening. Raindrops were beating against the windowpane in a miniature tattoo. Firmly closing her mind to the prospect of a hot bath, Marcia rummaged through her closet. Lucy always had been too intuitive for comfort. So the persona of the Marcia she had always been was going to be firmly in place. Cool, competent Marcia, in control of her own life. Unemotional, detached Marcia, who never made demands.

All her movements neat and efficient, she stripped off her work clothes, had a quick shower and dressed in a navy blue linen suit whose tailored elegance was worth every penny she had paid for it. Silky navy hose, Italian leather pumps and discreet gold jewelry came next. Expertly she applied her make-up. Then she brushed her sleek dark hair, in its expensive cut that curved just below her ears, and checked her appearance in the full-length mirror in her bedroom.

She didn't look thirty-three.

Not that it really mattered how old she looked.

Hastily she jammed her big horn-rimmed glasses on her nose. She could have worn her contacts. But her glasses gave her something to hide behind—and to meet Lucy she needed all the help she could get. Grabbing her shiny forest-green raincoat and still-damp umbrella from the hall closet, she left her condo and took the elevator to the basement.

She'd go straight to the gallery, meet the famous Quentin Ramsey, make appreciative noises about every one of his multiple personalities and invite Lucy and Troy to dinner on Sunday along with the rest of the family. And then she'd come home, duty done.

Multiple Personalities, she thought crossly, backing out of her parking lot. What kind of a name was that for a bunch of paintings? Too clever by half. Too cutesy. Altogether too self-conscious. He might be Lucy and Troy's friend, but that didn't mean that she, Marcia, had to like him.

Scowling, she pressed the remote control to open the garage door, and drove out into the rainswept evening.

Quentin, too, had checked his appearance in the mirror before he'd left for the art gallery. The amount of money he'd had to spend to get a decent suit that he planned to wear no more than half a dozen times a year had astounded him. He looked like an ad in a glossy men's magazine, he thought irritably, hitching at the knot in his silk tie: "The Successful Artist of the 90s. Man-about-town Quentin Ramsey attending the opening of his highly successful show *Multiple Personalities*."

What in hell had possessed him to come up with that title?

He ran a comb through his thick black curls, which instantly went right back to their usual state of disarray. He grinned at himself, feeling somewhat more cheerful. At least his hair refused to do the correct thing. And he'd always hated openings. Hated them with a passion.

He painted to communicate—no doubt about that. He didn't want his works stashed away in a studio with their faces to a wall. But he couldn't stand to hear people discussing them, stereotyping them, analyzing all their

vitality out of existence with words like "deconstruc-
tionism" and "postmodern abstractionism". At least the
critics had had to come up with some new labels for this
show, he thought, grinning again. Time he shook them
up a bit.

Someone would be bound to tell him that his new style
was a cop-out in the interests of commercialism. And
someone else would be sure to praise his raw honesty.
For some reason his kind of honesty was nearly always
called raw.

Speaking of which, he'd forgotten to eat anything.

Quentin went to the minibar and pilfered its entire
stock of peanuts and pretzels. Chewing absently, he
realized how much he was looking forward to seeing Lucy
and Troy. He'd turned down their invitation to dinner
because he had to be at the gallery early. But, if he had
his way, he'd end up the evening at the apartment they'd
rented and he'd take off his tie and his shiny leather
shoes that were already pinching his feet, and toss back
a beer or two. And he'd be sure to admire the new baby.
He knew rather more than most people what that baby
meant to them.

And as soon as he could he'd get out of Ottawa. Too
tidy a city for him. Too prettified. He wanted pine trees
and running water and maybe a mountain or two.

Not a hotel room—no matter how luxurious.

He opened the second bag of pretzels. What he really
needed to do was take a break from painting and build
another house. The bite of saw into lumber, the sweet
smell of wood chips, the satisfaction of seeing a roofline
cut into the sky—they all anchored him to a reality very
different from that of paint on canvas. It was a reality
he was beginning to crave.

There was nothing new about this. In his travels
around the world Quentin had always alternated periods
of intense artistic activity with the more mundane and

comforting reality of house construction. What was new was that the house he wanted to build this time was a house for himself. His own walls. His own roof.

He glanced at his watch and gave an exclamation of dismay. Grabbing his raincoat, he ran for the elevator, and in the lobby of the hotel hailed a cab. But as he was driven through the gleaming wet streets, still chewing on the pretzels, his thoughts traveled with him. He wanted to settle down. He'd been a nomad ever since he'd left his parents' yard at the age of three to follow the milk truck down the road, but now he wanted to have a place that he could call home.

It had been a long time since that little boy had stumbled along the dirt ruts, hollering at the milkman to wait for him. He was thirty-six now. And while he wanted a home, there was more to it than that. He wanted a woman to share that home. To share his home. His bed. His life. But she had to be the right woman.

He gazed vaguely at the beds of tulips that edged the road, neat blocks of solid color that moved him not at all. He'd been considerably older than three—eleven, perhaps—when he'd come to the conclusion that he'd know the woman he was meant to marry from the first moment he saw her. He knew perfectly well where that conviction had come from. His parents had had—he now realized, as an adult—the kind of marriage that happens only rarely. A marriage alive with love, laughter and passion, with fierce conflicts and an honesty that could indeed have been called raw.

He hadn't been able to verbalize this at age eleven, but he had intuited that there was something very special between the man and woman who were his parents. One of the often-told stories of his childhood had been how they had fallen in love at first sight, recognizing each other instantly as the partner each had been waiting for.

At the age of twenty-five, impatient, he'd ignored that certainty and married Helen. And within six weeks had known that he'd done the wrong thing. He'd hung in to the very best of his ability, and when she'd left him for a bank president twice her age had heaved a sigh of relief and vowed never to repeat that particular mistake.

Quentin was not a vain man, and it never ceased to surprise him that women flocked to him like blue jays to a feeder on a cold winter's day. Tall women, short women, beautiful women, sexy women. But not one of them so far had touched his soul.

What if he never found this mythical woman? Was he a fool to believe in the romantic dream of an eleven-year-old?

Maybe if he built the house first she'd somehow follow, as naturally as sunrise was bound to follow sunset.

Or maybe he was a fool even to think of settling down. He'd always rather prided himself on being a free spirit, going where he pleased when he pleased and staying as long as he pleased. If he got married, he wouldn't be able to do that.

The right woman...did she even exist?

He tried to wrench his mind away from thoughts that were, he'd sometimes concluded, both non-productive and infantile. The taxi swished through a puddle and drew up outside the gallery. Pots of scarlet tulips decorated the sidewalk, standing stiff and tall in the rain, like valiant soldiers on watch. I'm lonely, Quentin thought with a flash of insight. Despite my success, despite the incredible freedom of the way I live, I'm lonely.

"Ten seventy-five, sir," said the cabbie.

With a jerk Quentin came back to the present. He fumbled for the fare, added a tip, and ran for the gallery door. He wasn't all that free. Because he'd rather be walking the wet streets tonight than going to his own opening.

The owner of the gallery was a woman in her fifties, wife of a senior government official and dauntingly efficient; Quentin always wanted to call her Mrs. Harrington-Smythe rather than Emily—a name that did not suit her in the slightest. As he hung up his raincoat she gave his suit a quick appraisal and nodded her approval.

Wishing he'd left the price tag pinned to the cuff, Quentin allowed himself to be whisked on a tour of the gallery. Her placement of the paintings was all he could have asked; he only wished that they didn't make him feel as though he was about to undress in public. Emily gave him a copy of the catalog and ran through a list of the most prominent ministers, several deputy ministers and a sprinkling of diplomats.

Not bad for a kid from a little village in New Brunswick, thought Quentin, and did his best to memorize the names. Then the doorbell rang and he steeled himself to get through the next hours without abandoning the good manners his mother had worked very hard to instill in him.

Three-quarters of an hour later the place was humming. Eleven paintings had sold, the bartenders had been run off their feet and Quentin had been extremely civil to the first of the cabinet ministers—who didn't approve of anything painted after 1900 and wasn't backward in expressing his views. Then, from behind him, Quentin heard a woman call his name. He turned, gathered Lucy into his arms and hugged her hard. "Wonderful to see you!"

She said softly, "I can't believe you were being so polite—is this the Quentin I know?"

"I'm on my best behavior. You look gorgeous, Lucy—that's quite a dress."

Its purple folds made her mahogany curls glisten, and its *décolletage* verged on the indiscreet. "I thought you'd

like it," she said complacently. "Troy picked it out for
me."

Troy clapped Quentin on the shoulder. "Good to see
you. When this affair is over, we want you to come back
to the apartment so we can catch up on all the news."

"Done," said Quentin. "As long as you've got some
beer."

"Bought a twelve-pack this afternoon."

Troy was two or three inches taller than Quentin's five-
feet eleven, blond where Quentin was dark, and a medical
doctor rather than an artist; but from the time they had
met on Shag Island off the coast of Nova Scotia the two
men had liked one another. And when Quentin pictured
the home he was going to build for himself it was always
situated somewhere on the west coast within reach of
Vancouver.

Emily was fast approaching, with a man in tow who
looked like cabinet minister number two. Quentin raised
his brow at Lucy. "Duty calls. Talk to you later."

"We'll give you our address before we leave." Tucking
her arm into Troy's, she headed for the works in acrylic
that were such a break from the abstracts he had been
doing on the island.

The second cabinet minister asked several penetrating
questions and listened with genuine interest to Quentin's
replies. Then Quentin suffered through a very rich widow
with fake eyelashes who simply didn't understand the
first thing about art, and an importer of foreign cars
who understood only too well and insisted on inflicting
his theories on the artist. Quentin finally got rid of him
and headed for the bar. The pretzels had made him
thirsty.

He had just taken a gulp of what was a quite decent
Cabernet, hoping it would inspire him to plunge back
into the mêlée, when the door was pushed open once
again. Idly he watched as a woman walked into the foyer.

She closed her umbrella, shook water from it and straightened, the light falling on her face and the smooth swing of her hair. Dark hair that shone like polished wood.

Oh, Lord, thought Quentin. It's happened. At a gallery opening, of all places. That's her. The woman I've been waiting for.

He plunked his glass on the counter and pushed past several people who all wanted to speak to him, deaf to their remarks. The woman was hanging her dark green raincoat on the rack by the door, all her movements economical and precise. She's not my type, he thought blankly. Look at that suit. And those godawful glasses. What in heaven's name's going on here?

He was still ten feet away from her. She turned, taking the glasses from her nose and rubbing the rain from them with a tissue from her pocket, her face composed as she surveyed the crowded room. She might not be his type, but she was utterly, beguilingly beautiful.

His heart was banging in his chest like the ring of a hammer on boards. Feeling as clumsy as an adolescent, Quentin closed the distance between them and croaked, "I don't believe we've met."

She was no more than five feet five and delicately made, so that he felt large and clumsy. Her irises were the deep velvety purple of pansies and her lashes dark and thick; her bone structure was exquisite and her make-up flawless. Last of all, he saw how very soft and kissable was her mouth, and he felt his heart give another uncomfortable thud in his chest. She said in faint puzzlement, "Are you the gallery owner? I thought—"

"I'm the artist."

Her lashes flickered over unmistakable hostility. "Quentin Ramsey?"

He nodded. "And you?"

"Surely you don't meet everyone at the door?"

"You're the first."

"And to what," Marcia said silkily, "do I owe that honor?"

"Stop talking like a nineteenth-century novel. It doesn't suit you."

So much for the aristocratic British accent, thought Marcia. Not to mention the British good manners. "How can you possibly have any idea what suits me—I could be a professor of Victorian literature for all you know. Are you always so rude to potential customers?"

But Quentin was frowning, struggling to anchor a memory. "I've seen you somewhere. I'm sure I have."

"That's one of the oldest lines in the book."

"You cheapen both of us by that kind of remark."

"Oh, pardon me," she said. "In my experience, men—"

"I *have* seen you before."

"You're quite wrong—I've never met you." Because I would have remembered you, thought Marcia, trying to calm down. For the blue of your eyes, if nothing else. The deepest blue I've ever seen. Deep enough to lose myself.

"What's your name?"

She took a deep breath. Her imaginary portrait of Quentin Ramsey couldn't have been more inaccurate. This was definitely no tweed-jacketed Englishman who painted pretty landscapes under the influence of a great master. This man was a rugged individualist if ever she'd met one. Rugged, indeed; he looked as though he'd be more at home with a chainsaw than a paintbrush. She said coolly, "Dr. Marcia Barnes."

"*What*? You're Lucy's sister?"

He looked as shocked as though she'd just thrown a glass of wine in his face. She said, wondering why she should feel so angry, "We're very different, Lucy and I."

"No kidding. But that's why I thought I'd met you—Lucy has a photo of you in her living room." Fighting down a tumble of emotions that had an acute disappointment chief among them, Quentin said, 'You're the immunologist.'

"Yes."

Glaring at her, he demanded, "Why haven't you bothered visiting them since the baby was born?"

"I did! Last November."

"Sure—you managed to stay for two whole hours on your way to a medical conference. I said *visit*."

"It's really none of your—"

"When a conference is more important to you than your own family, you're in a bad way. Lucy's told me about you. 'Workaholic' is one way to describe you."

With studied charm Emily Harrington-Smythe said, "Quentin, may I borrow you for a few minutes? Mr. Brace has a couple of questions for you before he purchases the largest of the acrylics." She directed a polite smile at Marcia. "If you'll excuse us, please?"

"With pleasure," Marcia said crisply.

Determined to have the last word, Quentin announced, "Your sister and brother-in-law are in the other room. If you can spare the time, that is."

Seething, Marcia watched him cross the room and plunge into the crowd. His black hair was too long, curling at his nape, but at least those penetrating blue eyes were no longer pinning her to the wall. Just who did he think he was, daring to criticize her within moments of meeting her?

Deftly she secured a glass of wine at the bar. Lucy must have complained to him about that visit. It had been short, no question. But she'd just attended a conference on AIDS and had been on her way to another on immunodeficiency syndrome, and an afternoon had been all she could spare.

Even less anxious to meet her sister now, Marcia began to circle the room, turning her attention to the paintings. Within moments any thoughts of Lucy were banished from her mind. The works on this wall were all abstracts—some monochromatic, some boldly hued—and their emotional intensity tapped instantly into all the emptiness and confusion that she was beginning to realize she had been carrying around for quite a long time. The threat of losing her job had made them worse. But it hadn't given birth to them.

Eventually she found herself in front of a work titled *Composition Number 8*, whose vibrant spirals of color pulled her into their very depths. Her throat closed with pain. She'd never experienced what the immediacy of those colors symbolized: the joy, the passion, the fervent commitment—moment by moment—to the business of being alive. Never. And now maybe it was too late. Panic-stricken, she thought, I can't cry here. Not in a roomful of strangers.

I never cry.

"Are you all right?"

She would have known the voice anywhere. Trying to swallow the lump that was lodged tight against her voice box, Marcia muttered, "Go away."

A tear was hanging on her lashes. The sight of it piercing him to the heart, Quentin said flatly, "I'm sorry I was so rude to you. You're right. What's between you and Lucy is none of my business."

Orange, yellow, a flare of scarlet; the colors shimmered in Marcia's gaze, swirling together like the glowing heart of a fire that would burn her to a crisp were she to approach it. With an incoherent exclamation Quentin seized her by the arm, urged her toward a door near the corner of the room and opened it, pushing her inside. He snapped the door shut and said, "Now you can cry your eyes out—no one will see you here."

You will, she thought, and tugged her arm free. "I'm not crying. I never cry!"

"Then you must be allergic to paint. Your eyes are watering and your nose is running. Here."

He was holding out an immaculate white handkerchief. Marcia said the first thing that came into her head. "You don't look like the kind of man who'd go in for white handkerchiefs."

If she'd been looking at him rather than at the handkerchief, she would have seen his eyes narrow. "What kind of man do I look like?"

Blinking back tears that she still didn't want to acknowledge, Marcia glanced up. "When I was a little girl I used to play with paper dolls. You know the kind I mean? Cardboard cutouts that you put different outfits on with little paper tabs. Your suit looks like that—as though it's been stuck on you. With no regard for the kind of man you are. You should be wearing a sweatshirt and jeans. Not a pure wool suit and a Gucci tie."

"I'll have you know I spent a small fortune on this suit."

She said recklessly, "And begrudged every cent of it."

He threw back his head and laughed. "How true!"

Marcia's jaw dropped. His throat was strongly muscled and his teeth were perfect. Even his hair seemed to crackle with energy. This was the man who had created that painting—all those vivid colors suffused with a life force beyond her imagining. She took a step backward, suddenly more frightened than she'd been when the director had announced the cutbacks. More frightened than she could ever remember being. "The suit fits you perfectly," she said lamely. "I didn't mean to be rude."

It did fit him perfectly. But it still gave the impression of shoulder muscles straining at the seams, of a physique all the more impressive for being so impeccably garbed.

She took another step back. "You're not at all what I expected."

"Nor were the paintings," Quentin said shrewdly.

She didn't want to talk about the paintings. She took a tissue and a mirror from her purse, dabbed her nose, checked her mascara and said, "We should go back—you'll be missed."

He wasn't going to let her go that easily. "Why did that particular painting make you cry?"

Because it's what I've been missing all my life. Because it filled me with a bitter regret. Because it was as though you knew me better than I know myself. She said aloud, fighting for composure, "If you and Lucy have talked about me, you know I'm a very private person. My reaction is my own affair. Not yours."

Certainly Lucy had talked about Marcia. Not a lot, but enough for Quentin to realize that although Lucy loved her sister, she didn't feel close to her. He had gained a picture of a woman utterly absorbed in her work to the exclusion of her family and of intimacy. A cold woman who would do the right thing out of principle, not out of love, refusing to involve herself in all the joys and tragedies of everyday life.

And this was the woman he'd been waiting to meet for the last ten years? Or—more accurately—the last twenty-five? His intuition was giving him that message. Loud and clear. But maybe it was wrong.

He'd made a mistake when he'd ignored his intuition to marry Helen. Could he be making another—if different—mistake now? Had he willed Marcia into existence just because of his own needs? Because he was lonely?

"Why are you staring at me like that?" Marcia said fretfully.

Quentin made an effort to pull himself together. "The woman Lucy described to me wasn't the kind of woman who'd start to cry because some guy streaked paint on a piece of canvas."

Marcia wasn't sure what made her angrier—that Lucy had talked about her to Quentin or that his words were so accurate. "Oh, wasn't she? What—?"

A peremptory rap came on the door. Much relieved, Marcia said, "Your public awaits you. You'd better go, Mr. Ramsey."

"Quentin. Are you going to Lucy and Troy's place when this shindig is over?"

"I am not."

The door opened and Emily Harrington-Smythe poked her head in. "Quentin? I really need you out here."

"I'll be right there." He reached out and took the glasses from Marcia's nose. "You have truly beautiful eyes. Who are you hiding from?"

"From people as aggressive as you."

She grabbed for the glasses. Laughter glinting in his own eyes, he evaded her. "You can have them back if you promise to have lunch with me tomorrow."

"I'm sure any number of women in this gallery would be delighted to have lunch with you—but I'm not one of them."

"I'll wear my jeans."

His smile was very hard to resist. Marcia resisted it with all her will power. "My glasses, please."

"I'll get your phone number from Lucy."

"My telephone displays the number of the person calling me. If I think it's you, I won't answer."

"It'll take more than modern technology to defeat me, Dr. Marcia Barnes. Because you still haven't told me why my painting made you cry." He passed her the glasses and dropped a kiss on the tip of her nose. "See you around."

He strode out of the room. For the space of five minutes he hadn't felt the least bit lonely. Taking Emily by the arm, he said urgently, "*Composition Number 8* in the catalog—I want you to put a 'Not for Sale' sign on it."

Emily said bluntly, "I can't do that. Not when it's listed."

"Then mark it 'Sold'."

"It's not," Emily said with indisputable logic.

"It is. I'm buying it."

"Quentin, what's wrong with you? I've never seen you behave so erratically at an opening."

"I'm buying *Number 8*," he repeated patiently. "There's nothing particularly erratic about that."

"You can't buy your own painting! Anyway, Mr. Sorensen has his eye on it, and he wields a lot of influence in this city."

"Too bad. Mr. Sorensen isn't getting it. I am."

"But—"

"Do it, Emily," Quentin said with a pleasant smile. "If you want another Quentin Ramsey show next year."

His shows were enormously successful financially. "Very well," Emily said huffily. "But I'll have to charge you the full commission."

"After tonight I'm sure I can afford it," he said. "That looks like the last of the cabinet ministers. I'll go and do my bit."

Trying to push out of his mind the image of a woman's long-lashed violet eyes swimming in tears, wondering how she'd react when he presented her with an extremely expensive painting, he made his way toward the man in the gray pin-striped suit.

CHAPTER TWO

MARCIA stayed behind in the room that she now decided must be the gallery owner's office, struggling to subdue a mixture of rage at Quentin's effrontery and a truant amusement at his persistence. Mr. Quentin Ramsey, she'd be willing to bet, wasn't used to women who said no. Not that she'd been playing games with him. She was in enough trouble at work, without adding a man who asked questions she didn't want to answer, who had blue eyes that seemed to burn their way into her very soul and who was—she could admit it now that she was alone—sexual dynamite.

It wasn't just his body, its hard planes ill-concealed by his tailored suit. His fingers were long and sensitive, the backs of his hands taut with sinews, and his face with its strong bones had character more than standard good looks—a character hinting at the complexities of the man within. It was an inhabited face, she thought slowly, the face of a man who'd tasted deeply of life, experiencing its dark side as well as its light.

She'd noticed an awful lot in a very few minutes. Too much for her own peace of mind. Altogether too much.

Every instinct she possessed urged her to head straight for the coat rack and leave. But if she did so Lucy and Troy would have a fit. She squared her shoulders and marched back into the gallery, purposely not looking at the painting so unimaginatively called *Composition Number 8*.

She picked out Quentin immediately; he was talking to a man in a pin-striped suit with every evidence of courteous attention. But then his eyes swiveled to meet hers, as though he'd sensed her standing there watching him. He winked at her. Marcia tilted her chin, turned her back and headed for the far gallery.

Lucy and Troy were gazing at a small work in one corner. Troy had his arm draped around Lucy's shoulders while Lucy's body language said more clearly than words that the man holding her was the man she adored. Again hot tears flooded Marcia's eyes. I've got to stop this, she thought frantically. Right now. I've avoided marriage and commitment like the plague. So why does the sight of my sister's happiness make me feel like a failure? Smarten up, Marcia!

She made a gallant effort to gather the shreds of the control for which she was so famous. Then, her lips set, her chin high, she said casually, "Hi, Lucy... Troy."

Lucy whirled, ducking out of the circle of Troy's arm. "Marcia—I'm so pleased to see you!"

Marcia had never encouraged hugging. Lucy contented herself with kissing her sister on the cheek and Troy brushed his lips in the vicinity of her other cheek. Then Lucy stood back, scrutinizing her sister. "You look tired," she said. "Are you all right?"

Exactly the question Quentin had asked. "I'm fine— I've been exceptionally busy at work. What do you think of the show?"

"There are four silkscreen prints on the other wall that I lust after. And I think the acrylics are brilliant—such a departure." Lucy put her head to one side. "This one, for instance—it's a jewel."

In exquisite detail Quentin had painted three little girls running through a meadow full of wildflowers; it was a tribute to his talent that the work was entirely without sentimentality. "They look like us," Marcia blurted.

"Oh... I hadn't thought of that. You and I and Cat, you mean. You're right—two brunettes and a redhead!"

Lucy laughed. "Maybe he saw the photo I have of the three of us on the piano."

"Would you like to have it?" Troy asked, his slate-gray eyes resting affectionately on his wife.

"*I* would," Marcia heard herself say.

Lucy was gazing at her speculatively and Troy's eyebrows had shot halfway up his forehead. Aghast, Marcia sputtered, "I didn't really mean that—I don't want it, of course I don't. You get it, Lucy."

"Have you met Quentin?" Lucy asked.

"Yes. Very briefly. Please, Lucy, forget I ever said I wanted it. Buy her the painting, Troy."

"I'll get it for you, sis," Troy said. "I didn't give you anything for your last birthday."

"But we never give each other expensive presents!"

"This will be the exception that proves the rule... I'll be right back."

And Marcia, for the third time that evening, found her eyes brimming with tears. Lucy drew her further into the corner, shielding her from the other guests. "You're not yourself—what's wrong?"

"Nothing. Everything. *I* don't know."

"Have lunch with me tomorrow."

"I can't. I've got to go into work."

"Darn your work, Marcie!"

Lucy only used Marcia's childhood name when she was upset. Marcia said, "I'm going to phone Mother in the morning—could you and Troy come for dinner on Sunday? Catherine's free."

"Love to," Lucy said promptly.

"Come around six, then... I do wish Troy wasn't buying me that painting."

"Too bad we can't take it home right away. It'd look perfect in your bedroom."

A painting of Quentin Ramsey's in her bedroom? No way, thought Marcia, and from the corner of her eye saw Emily Harrington-Smythe parting the crowd with Troy in her wake. "An excellent choice," Emily said, sticking a little red circle beside the painting. "Congratulations, Dr. Donovan."

"Happy birthday, Marcia," Troy said, with a lazy grin at his sister-in-law.

The painting was hers. Whether she wanted it or not. Standing on tiptoes, Marcia kissed Troy on the chin and said limpidly, "Thank you, Troy, that was sweet of you."

"Let's go and find Quentin and tell him what we've done," he rejoined.

In sheer panic Marcia said, "I've really got to go—I was in the lab at six this morning. But I'll see you both on Sunday." Giving them a quick smile, she almost ran from the room.

Quentin was standing in the far corner of the gallery with three very attractive women—two of them blondes, the other a voluptuous creature with glorious black curls. He was laughing at something one of them had said. Marcia pulled on her coat, picked up her umbrella and scurried out into the rain.

Marcia's mother, Dr. Evelyn Barnes, was a forensic pathologist, a poised and gracious hostess and a demon golfer. But when Marcia phoned her from work the next morning, Evelyn sounded unusually flustered.

"Dinner? On Sunday? With the family? Let me get my book... I—Marcia, could I bring someone with me? A friend?"

"Of course. Is Lillian in town?"

Lillian was her mother's best friend, who had moved to Toronto only a month ago. "No—no, it's not Lillian. It's a man."

Evelyn always had an escort to the concerts and dinner parties she frequented, but never allowed these undoubtedly very fine men to mingle with her family. "You're being a dark horse, Mother. What's his name?"

"Henry Woods. He's a broker. I—I'd like you to meet him."

Trying very hard to hit a balance between unmannerly curiosity and diplomatic uninterest, Marcia said soothingly, "That's just fine. Six o'clock?"

"Lovely. We'll see you then." Evelyn, who usually liked to catch up on all the family news, smartly cut the connection.

More slowly, Marcia put the receiver down. If she didn't know better, she'd say her mother was in love. Her cool, unemotional mother in love?

It didn't look as though her dinner party would be dull.

At five to six on Sunday Marcia was putting the finishing touches to her make-up. The same perverse instinct that had caused her to claim the painting of the three little girls had induced her to ignore the elegant but rather dull outfits that made up the bulk of her wardrobe, as well as her horn-rimmed glasses. She was wearing black stirrup pants with a long black sweater emblazoned with the golden face of a lion; her pumps were black with gold buckles. Despite the addition of the mysterious Mr. Woods, this was only a family dinner, she thought defiantly, adding scarlet lipstick and big gold earrings that dangled against her neck. Besides, it had rained all weekend.

The security buzzer sounded and Lucy's voice came over the intercom. A few moments later there was a tap on the door. Before Marcia could say anything, Lucy handed her sister the baby so she could take off her coat and said ingenuously, "We brought Quentin along. I hope you don't mind? The cocktail party he was supposed to go to was canceled because the hostess had the flu.''

Christopher Stephen Donovan grabbed at Marcia's earrings and drooled down the shoulder of her sweater. Quentin's eyes were even bluer than she remembered them. Marcia backed up so that they could come in and mumbled untruthfully, ''No, that's fine. No problem at all.''

Lucy handed Troy her coat and swiped at Lucy's shoulder with a tissue. ''He's teething again—I keep telling Troy someone should invent a better method for the acquiring of teeth. Here, I'll take him now.''

But Christopher had locked his arms around Marcia's neck and burrowed his face into her shoulder. He smelled sweetly of baby powder and warm skin, his weight solid against her body. Her arms tightened around him as she rested her cheek on his wispy hair. Oh God, she thought helplessly, here I go again. I want to weep my eyes out. I'm cracking up. I've never wanted children. Not once in my thirty-three years.

Quentin, meanwhile, had been hanging up his coat and combing the raindrops from his hair—more to give himself time to collect his wits than from any urge for neatness. His first glimpse of Marcia in all that black and gold had sent a jolt through his system as though he'd grabbed a live wire; he'd simultaneously wanted to look his fill and throw her down on the carpet and kiss her senseless. Then Lucy had given her the baby, and, as though the carpet had moved beneath his feet, he'd seen her holding his child, their child, the fruit of their love.

You're nuts, he told himself astringently. She hasn't even agreed to have lunch with you and you're already into fatherhood? He said, ''Marcia, I brought you these. They were selling them at the market.''

Marcia looked up. He was clutching a large, inartistic bouquet of mixed flowers—oranges clashing with pinks, purple next to magenta. His gaze locked with hers and she found herself quite unable to look away. "Thank you," she said breathlessly. "Lucy can show you where to find a vase."

"Left my suit back at the hotel," he added.

He looked extremely handsome in soft-fitting gray cords and a dark blue sweater. "I see," Marcia said inanely.

Quentin handed the bouquet to Lucy and stepped closer to Marcia. "He's going to pull your hair out by the roots... Let go, Chris." Then she felt the warmth of a man's fingers against her nape and felt his breath stir her hair. Every nerve in her body sprang to jangling life. Her shoulders rigid, her breathing caught in her throat, she heard Chris mumble a protest; his little fist tightened on her hair and she winced.

"Easy, Chris... there we go."

With infinite gentleness Quentin had loosened the baby's hold. As he eased the child out of her arms his forearm brushed her breast. The shock ran through her body; he must have felt it. She flashed a desperate glance around and saw that Troy and Lucy were watching her with considerable interest. I will not blush. I will not, she told herself. She said in a strangled voice, "I've got to keep an eye on the dinner. I'll be right back."

Troy started setting up their portable playpen, Quentin swung baby Chris high over his head so that he gurgled with laughter, and Lucy followed Marcia into the kitchen. "Is Mother coming? Yummy—something smells delicious."

Glad to talk about anything other than Quentin, Marcia said, "She's bringing a man," and relayed the gist of the phone call. Before she'd finished Catherine arrived and sauntered into the kitchen, and she had to go through her story again.

Dr. Catherine Barnes was petite like Marcia, elegant like their mother, and did research in pancreatic cancer. "I'm on holiday for three whole weeks," she crowed. "I'm looking after Lydia's dogs next week, so I'll get lots of exercise and fresh air. You look like you could do with some sun, Marcia, you're much too pale."

Cat was a fitness freak who could always be counted on to say it like it was. "Thanks," Marcia said drily. "But it does happen to have been raining for the last four days—or hadn't you noticed? Would you pass around the crab dip, Cat? And I'll get Troy to pour drinks."

Lucy had jammed the flowers in Marcia's largest vase. "Where'll I put them?"

Quentin was standing in the kitchen doorway, minus Chris. "I'll put them in the middle of the table," he said.

Marcia had placed an attractive arrangement of silk flowers that matched her china as a centerpiece. She watched Quentin plunk it on the sideboard and put the motley bouquet in its place. He was exactly the kind of man she disliked—making decisions without consulting her, taking over as though he owned the place. As he came back in the kitchen she said frostily, "The only thing missing from that bouquet is skunk cabbage."

"Better luck next time."

"Next time? You don't look the type to enjoy city life. I can't imagine you're going to stay in Ottawa for long."

"I wasn't going to—but I've changed my plans," he said. "A friend of mine who's away owns a place in the Gatineau Hills, so I'm going to stay there for a while. You and I still have to have lunch—or had you forgotten?"

"You're very sure of yourself, Mr. Ramsey."

"Confidence gets results, Dr. Barnes."

"Up until now confidence might have gotten you results," she said sweetly.

"Are you suggesting I should change tactics?"

"I'm suggesting you abandon the project."

"I don't think so. You're an interesting challenge."

Her nostrils flared. "Now you're being insulting."

He stepped closer and said softly, "You liked it when I touched you."

Gritting her teeth, Marcia thought about icebergs and glaciers and Scotch on the rocks, and her cheeks stayed only as pink as the heat of the stove warranted. "You took me by surprise, that's all. A man of your experience should be more adept at distinguishing between a woman who's startled and a woman who's ready to fall at your feet."

Quentin was by now thoroughly enjoying himself. "Dear me . . . a woman has never once thrown herself at my feet. Does that make me a failure as a man? Although it does sound rather a deranged thing to— Oh, thanks, Troy. I'll have a beer."

Had Troy been listening? Appalled, Marcia said stiffly, "You'll have to excuse me . . . Oh, there's the buzzer— that must be Mother."

Evelyn Barnes looked very attractive in her rose-pink dress with her gray hair softly curling round her ears. Her usual escorts were tall, patrician-featured men, who considered themselves essential to the running of the country; Henry Woods was short, stout, bald and unassuming, with a pair of the kindest brown eyes Marcia had ever seen. She warmed to him immediately. She made introductions all around, Troy passed the drinks, and Marcia set a place for Quentin at the table, seating him where the flowers would screen him from her view.

Two and a half hours later Marcia was plugging in the coffee-machine in the kitchen. She was pleased with the success of her dinner party. Quentin and Henry had proved to be witty and entertaining, Cat had thrown off her normal reserve and the baby had filled any gaps in the conversation. As for herself, she'd managed to avoid anything but minimal contact with Quentin. He couldn't move out to the Gatineau Hills fast enough for her.

She reached in the refrigerator for the cream. But the container was almost empty and she'd forgotten to buy a new one. She went back in the living room. Troy and Quentin were getting out the chess pieces while Evelyn was giving Chris his bottle. "I'll have to run to the corner store—I'm out of cream," Marcia said. "Won't be a minute."

Quentin got to his feet. "I'll come with you. I need to walk off some of that excellent dinner."

She couldn't very well tell him to get lost. Evelyn wouldn't approve of that. So Marcia got her purse, pulled on shiny black boots and her raincoat and went out into the hall with him. His belted trenchcoat gave him the air of a particularly rakish spy.

"Let's take the stairs," Quentin said. "I shouldn't have had a second helping of that chocolate dessert—deadly."

"It was only Belgian chocolate, whipping cream and butter," Marcia said, wide-eyed. "Oh, and six eggs too."

"It should be against medical ethics to make caffeine and cholesterol taste so good."

"It's Cat's favorite dessert. That article she told us about was interesting, wasn't it?"

But Quentin hadn't braved the rain to talk about Cat. As they went outside he opened Marcia's umbrella, held it over their heads and pulled her close to his side, tucking her arm in his. "There," he said. "Alone at last."

His strong-boned face was only inches from hers; his gaze was intent. She said coolly, "This is a big city— we're scarcely alone."

"Don't split hairs, Marcia. There are just two people under this umbrella—tell the truth for once."

"All right, so we're alone. So what?"

"Why did my painting make you cry?"

"Quentin, I have guests who are waiting for their coffee—come along!"

"You're bright, you're competent, you're a dab hand with Belgian chocolate—and you're scared to death of your own emotions. That's quite a combination."

Besides a rum and cola before dinner, Marcia had had two glasses of red wine with dinner. She said, pulling her arm free as she turned to face him and wishing that the umbrella didn't cloister them quite so intimately, "You want the truth? I'll give you the truth. You're wasting your time, Quentin. I'm thirty-three years old—not fifteen. If I'm scared of emotion I presumably have adequate reasons, and if I'm as bright as you say I am they must be good reasons. I'm also much too old to be spilling out my life story to every man that comes along."

Quentin didn't like being bracketed with a procession of other men. He wanted to be different. He wanted to shake her up. As raindrops spattered on the umbrella he stroked the smooth fall of her hair with his free hand and said huskily, "You look like an Egyptian goddess in that outfit you're wearing."

Hot color flared in her cheeks. "I wouldn't have worn it if I'd known you were coming," she said, then could have bitten off her tongue.

He pounced. "You don't want me seeing the real you?"

"I don't know who the real me is anymore!" Marcia exclaimed, then rolled her eyes in self-disgust. "Telling the truth seems to be addictive. Quentin, it's pouring rain. Let's go."

"Maybe I call you to truth," he said quietly. Then he clasped her by the chin, lowered his head and kissed her full on the lips. Her lips weren't cold; they were so soft and desirable that he lost all track of time and place in the sheer pleasure of the moment. When she suddenly jerked her chin free, it came as a physical shock.

"You mustn't do that,' she gabbled. "You scarcely know me. You can't just go kissing me as if we're lovers in a Hollywood movie—and now you've got lipstick all over your mouth."

She sounded anything but unemotional, and her first, instinctive yielding had set his head swimming. Quentin fished in his pocket, producing another handkerchief. "You'd better wipe it off," he said.

"So that's why you carry a handkerchief—I should have known," she said nastily, and scrubbed at his lips with painful vigor.

He was suddenly angry out of all proportion. Pulling his head back, he said, "Let me tell you something— my dad was a lumberjack in a little village in New Brunswick that I'm sure you've never heard of—Holton, in the Kennebecasis Valley—and my mom cleaned the houses of the rich folk. A white handkerchief was the mark of a gentleman to her, and when I won a provincial art competition at the age of twelve she gave me six boxes of handkerchiefs. I may not qualify as a gentleman but I loved my mother, and that's why I always carry a white handkerchief."

Marcia stood very still. Water was dripping from the prongs of the umbrella and her feet were getting cold. She said, "I'm sorry—I shouldn't have said that."

She was looking straight at him, and her apology was obviously sincere. "Okay. But you really get under my skin, Marcia Barnes."

"That's mutual," she snorted, and wiped the last of the lipstick from the corner of his mouth. His nose was slightly crooked and there was a dent in his chin; his brows and lashes were as black as his hair. As for his

mouth... She shivered in a way that had nothing to do
with the cold. She had never been kissed like that in her
life. Brief, beautiful and bewildering, she thought,
tugging at his sleeve and starting off down the sidewalk,
even through his coat she could feel the hard muscles of
his arm.

They walked in silence for several minutes. Then
Quentin said abruptly, "Have dinner with me tomorrow
night."

"I can't."

"Tuesday, then."

"You'll be in the Gatineau Hills."

"I have a car. It's less than an hour's drive."

"The store where I can get the cream is in the bottom
floor of that apartment block—I won't be a minute,"
Marcia gasped, then darted from under the umbrella and
ran inside.

The harsh fluorescent lighting and the aisles packed
with food restored her to some kind of sanity. One kiss
and I would indeed have fallen at his feet, she realized
grimly, taking the container of cream out of the refrigerator and marching to the checkout. But just because my hormones are doing a dance like daffodils in
springtime doesn't mean I have to have dinner with the
man. In fact, it's precisely why I shouldn't have dinner
with him. I'm in enough of a muddle without adding a
wild card like Quentin Ramsey to the pack.

She paid for the cream and went outside. Quentin was
waiting for her, a tall, blue-eyed stranger standing under
a streetlamp. He did call her to truth, she thought unhappily. To truth and to emotion—a devastating combination for a woman used to hiding herself from both.
How was she going to convince him that she didn't want
to date him? Normally she had no trouble getting rid of
men who forced their attentions on her.

As she cudgeled her brains, he forestalled her. "If you're too busy at work to have dinner through the week, I can wait until next weekend."

Marcia bit her lip and started to walk back the way they'd come. "Quentin, I don't want to see you again. I'm sorry if that sounds harsh, but that's the way it is."

"Why not?"

She said childishly, "Because. Just because! Okay?"

"No, dammit, it's not okay! I know you're attracted to me, and I'm willing to bet you don't lose your cool with anyone else the way you have with me. My painting made you cry, your whole body responds when I touch you, and the more I see of you the more I figure Lucy doesn't have a clue what makes you tick." He drew a harsh breath. "Plus she told me how much you wanted the painting of the three little girls—the one Troy bought for you."

Spacing her words, Marcia seethed, "I can want a painting. That doesn't mean I have to have dinner with the artist. You're not a stupid man and that's not a very complicated message. So why aren't you getting it?"

"Because I don't want to," he said tightly. Although his features were inscrutable, Quentin was beginning to feel scared; any time he'd visualized finding the perfect woman she'd been as delighted to discover him as he her.

If Marcia had used her common sense she would have changed the subject. "I don't understand you—why are you pushing me so hard?" she cried.

"If I told you, you'd laugh in my face."

"Then please just drop it, Quentin."

"I can't!" He took a deep breath, trying to think. "I'm going to be seeing a fair bit of Troy and Lucy over the summer, so I'm bound to see you again. Unless you avoid them for the next two months, of course."

"I'll make sure when I go and see them that you're not included," she snapped.

"So you're not indifferent to me . . . If you were, you wouldn't care if I was there or not."

"I don't like being harassed."

His steps slowed. "That's an ugly word."

"Then don't do it."

Her jaw was set mutinously. The pale sweep of her cheekbones made him ache somewhere deep inside. He said desperately, "Marcia, I don't think I've ever begged a woman to spend time with me . . . I guess I've never had to. So if I'm not doing this well it's because I haven't had any practise. I'm begging you now. You're important to me in ways I don't understand but that I know to be real. Give me a chance—that's all I ask."

To her infinite relief she saw they'd reached the driveway to her building. It took all her courage to look up at him, and the torment in his face almost weakened her resolve. "There's no point—please believe me." She tried to smile. "I'm sorry."

She was right, she knew she was; she was being sensible and rational. She had never thought of herself as an overly adept judge of male character, but she was certain that any relationship with Quentin wouldn't be shallow. Better to end whatever was between them now rather than later.

So why was she filled with the same bitter regret that his painting had called up in her? And why did she feel as though she'd just trampled on a whole field of daffodils?

She stalked into the building and up the stairs, and before she unlocked her door forced a bright smile on her face.

The next two hours were purgatory. But finally Evelyn and Henry stood up and everyone else followed their lead.

Quentin pushed back his chair, trying to stretch the tension from his shoulders. Troy had trounced him royally at chess because his mind had been anywhere but on the game. His thoughts had been going round and round in circles that had ended up exactly nowhere. He should have kept his cool with Marcia. Kept things light and on the surface. Instead he'd kissed her before she was ready, and badgered her as if his sole intention had been to push her away.

For a man she'd said wasn't stupid, he'd sure blown it. Nor did he have any idea what he was going to do next. According to Marcia, there wasn't any next.

He was the last one to go out the door. Marcia shrank away from him, and he saw that there were faint blue shadows under her eyes. Filled with a passionate compunction, and another emotion that he wasn't quite ready to label fear, he said roughly, "If you change your mind, get in touch with me. You can always reach me through Lucy and Troy."

"Yes... yes, of course," she said, already starting to close the door.

She couldn't wait to be rid of him—that was the message. Quentin headed for the elevator where the rest of them were waiting, somehow made appropriate small talk until Troy dropped him off at the hotel and then headed for the bar. There were times in life when only a double rum would do.

CHAPTER THREE

THE following Sunday Marcia had lunch with Lucy. When they were settled in an alcove in the salad bar that was Lucy's favorite and they'd made their choices from the menu, Lucy took a sip of her wine and said with sisterly frankness, "You don't look so hot, Marcia."

Marcia knew that she didn't, and she knew why. Opting for part of the truth, because she certainly wasn't going to talk about Quentin, she said, "Last Tuesday I was called into the director's office and informed that due to budget restraints the junior staff are being required to take a week's holiday without pay. As soon as possible. So as of Friday afternoon I've been on vacation."

Lucy went right to the heart of the matter. "What does that do to your research?"

"The particular drugs I've been working with aren't available either—all of a sudden they're too expensive. So almost three months' work could go down the drain." Marcia grimaced in frustration. "It's driving me crazy."

"How secure is your job?" Lucy asked bluntly.

Marcia twirled the stem of her glass, not looking at her sister. "I might lose it," she said, and heard the telltale quiver in her voice.

Lucy reached a hand across the tablecloth. "Oh, Marcie..."

Marcia bit her lip. "It's crazy—there are lots of people much worse off than I am. But I really love my job." She took a big swallow of her wine. "They're supposed to make an announcement within two or three weeks."

38

Lucy said gently, "Your whole life revolves around your research."

"Stop it, Lucy, or I'll be blubbering all over you," Marcia said with a watery grin. "Have some bread."

"'Blubbering', as you put it, can be a perfectly fine response."

"Not in a crowded restaurant."

Lucy slathered butter on a slab of crunchy French bread. "I suppose you're right. So what will you do with yourself all week?"

"I'm not sure yet." Not for anything would she reveal to her sister that the thought of seven more days with absolutely nothing to do filled her with panic.

"I've got an idea! You can go to Quentin's cottage in the Gatineau Hills."

"Don't be silly," Marcia said sharply, her nerves shrilling like a burglar alarm at the sound of his name.

"He won't be there—it's perfect. He left for New York today. One of his works got vandalized in a gallery in SoHo, and he felt he had to go and see the damage himself. He said he wouldn't be back until Friday or Saturday."

She could get out of her condo and away from the city. "I never was much for the great outdoors," Marcia prevaricated.

"Troy and Chris and I were there all day yesterday— it's a beautiful spot on a lake, with lovely woods and wildflowers. And the cottage is luxurious. Not what you'd call roughing it."

"I couldn't do that without asking him, Lucy. And it's too late if he's already left."

"I'll take full responsibility—you see, he was hoping we'd stay there. But Troy gets his lunch hours free and a couple of afternoons through the week, and I like to spend all the time I can with him. So I'm sure it'd be fine with Quentin if you stayed at the cottage."

Marcia was sensitive enough to pick up what Lucy wasn't saying. Lucy and Troy's first child had died at the age of seven months—a tragedy that had ripped apart the fabric of their marriage; they had lived separately for over a year. Now that they were back together Lucy hated to be away from Troy, and, she had once confided to Marcia, she felt safer when Troy was near for Chris as well.

Marcia said spontaneously, "Chris is a sweetheart, Lucy."

A film of tears covered Lucy's gray-blue eyes. "Yes, he is—we're very lucky. Now that he's older than seven months, I feel so much more relaxed too—silly, isn't it?" She helped herself to another slice of bread. "Do you ever think you might want children?"

"What kind of a question's that?" Marcia said lightly.

"You looked very sweet holding Chris—even though he was dribbling all over you."

"I've never been a mother but I'm sure there's more to it than standing around looking sweet. How are Troy's courses going?"

"Fine. You didn't answer the question."

"I'm not going to. Because I don't know the answer."

Lucy stared at her thoughtfully. "You didn't hit it off with Quentin, did you?"

Marcia scowled. "Did you invite me out for lunch just so you could subject me to an inquisition?"

"Yes," said Lucy, with one of her insouciant grins.

The waitress gave Marcia her Greek salad and Lucy her seafood salad. "Can I get you anything else, ladies?"

"That's fine, thanks," Marcia said, and picked up her fork.

She was worried sick about her job—that was an undeniable fact. But there was another reason that she looked far from her best. And that reason was Quentin. She'd only met the man twice, but somehow he'd insinuated his way into her life, so that his rugged face came between her and the computer screen and his loose-limbed stride accompanied her down the corridors of the institute. At work, where she was so disciplined, she'd more or less managed to keep him in order. But at home in her condo it was another story.

She hadn't slept well all week. But when she did sleep she dreamed about Quentin, night after night. Sometimes they were dreams so erotic that she woke blushing, her whole body on fire with needs that even in the darkness she could scarcely bring herself to acknowledge as her own. But at other times she woke from nightmares—horrible nightmares that left her heart pounding with terror and her palms wet.

They were always the same: she was drowning in the sea, being pulled down and down into the deep blue depths of a bottomless and merciless ocean, and when she suddenly saw Quentin's face through the swirling currents and tried to signal to him to rescue her he was always out of reach, his black hair waving like seaweed, his smile full of mockery.

"I really don't want to talk about Quentin, Lucy," she said shortly.

Lucy, known for being impulsive, chewed on a mouthful of shrimp and said nothing. Marcia picked at her black olives and decided they'd used too much olive oil. She said at random, "What did you think of Mother's friend Henry?"

"I thought he was a sweetheart. Do you think she'll marry him?"

"Mother? Get married again? No!"

"She must get lonely sometimes. Troy and I live in Vancouver, and you and Cat are both very busy women."

"Workaholics, you mean," Marcia said drily. It was the word Quentin had used.

"I'm trying to be polite," Lucy chuckled. "Oh, Marcia, it's so neat that Troy and I are having a couple of months in Ottawa! I love Vancouver, and I don't have to tell you how much I love Troy and Chris—but I do miss my family."

It was the perfect opportunity for Marcia to say that she missed Lucy. But was it true? Or did Lucy, with her tumbled curls and her untidy emotions, simply stir Marcia up in ways she both resented and feared? "Families are complicated," she said obliquely.

"Mmm, that's true enough... You know, it's funny, but I really thought you and Quentin would like each other."

"Lay off, Lucy."

"When we saw him yesterday he looked as awful as you do. And he didn't want to talk about you any more than you want to talk about him."

"Then maybe you should take the hint."

"But he was such a good friend to me on Shag Island—I met him there, remember, when Troy and I were separated." Lucy speared another shrimp. "He was like the brother we never had."

Marcia could not possibly picture Quentin as her brother. She said flatly, "He's too intense for me—he came on too strong. I'm sorry I spoiled your fantasy, but there it is. Now, can we please talk about something—or someone—else?"

Lucy sighed. "Troy's always telling me I'm a hopeless romantic. Okay, okay—I'll drop it. But I will give you the key to the cottage and the directions. You should take your own food—Quentin's not what you'd call a model housekeeper. And, providing you leave there by Friday morning, there's no danger of you running into him. More's the pity."

Marcia glared at her. Lucy went on hurriedly, "Next Saturday why don't you come for dinner with Troy and

me and we'll go to a movie? Cat's offered to babysit.''
She gave a shamefaced smile. "I'm still not comfortable
leaving Chris with a sitter who doesn't have an MD after
her name. Silly, isn't it?''

"I think it's very understandable," Marcia said,
sharing the last of the carafe of wine between them.
"What movie do you want to see?''

As Lucy began discussing the merit of various new
releases Marcia found herself remembering the year that
Lucy had lived in Ottawa and then on Shag Island, and
Troy had lived in Vancouver; their unhappiness had been
a measure of the depth of their love—she hadn't been
so wrapped up in her own concerns that she hadn't
understood that. She had been helpless to fix what was
wrong, and that, too, had been a new experience. She
liked to feel in control of events.

Maybe, she thought slowly, that was the year when
she'd begun to sense the sterility of her own life; the
tragedy that had struck Lucy and Troy had been the
origin of a confusion and a lack of focus that was both
new to her and horribly unsettling.

And that made Quentin fifty times worse.

"There's that new historical movie too," she said.
"One of the technicians at work saw it and really liked
it.''

For the rest of their lunch they talked about anything
but family and men, although Marcia did find herself
clutching the key to the cottage and a map sketched on
a paper placemat when she went back to her car. And
why not? she thought rebelliously. If she spent all next
week in her condo, she'd be talking to the plants. A few
days beside a lake with lots of books and no people would
be just fine.

But she'd leave there Thursday evening, to make sure
that she didn't meet up with Quentin.

*   *   *

Marcia got away on Monday morning, her little gray car loaded with food, clothes, books and a portable TV. She drove along the eastern shore of the Gatineau River, humming to herself. How long since she'd done something like this? Too long. Her vacations tended to be carefully planned affairs with equally carefully chosen friends, not last-minute escapades all by herself.

She was going to read all the novels she'd bought in the last year that had been stashed on her shelves because she hadn't had time to get at them. She'd experiment with some new pasta recipes. She'd watch the shows she always missed on TV because something needed doing at the lab. She was going to have a great time.

Marcia got lost twice trying to follow the penciled squiggles on her sister's map; Lucy wasn't blessed with a sense of direction. But finally the little side road she had been following forked in two just as it was supposed to. When she took the right fork within three hundred yards she saw a wooden gate with a plaque attached to the post. "Richardson" it said. That was the name of Quentin's friends, the ones who owned the cottage.

Marcia got out, opened the gate, drove through and closed it behind her. Her car bumped down a lane overhung with newly leafed beech trees and red-tasseled maples. Then she emerged into a clearing and braked.

Through the lacy fretwork of the trees the lake sparkled and danced. A carpet of white trilliums patterned the forest floor. And the cottage—the cottage was beautiful.

It was a house more than a cottage, a cedar house with a wood-shingled roof and a broad stone chimney; it merged with its surroundings perfectly. Smiling fatuously, Marcia drove to the circle of gravel at the end of the driveway and parked her car.

Over the deep silence of the woods she could hear the ripple of the lake on the shore and a chorus of birdsong. The front of the house, which faced the lake, was made of panels of glass set in thick beams reaching to the peak of the roof. The tree trunks and the blue of the sky were reflected in the glass.

Like a woman in a dream she walked up the stone path to the front door. The key turned smoothly in the lock. She stepped inside and gave a gasp of dismay.

What had Lucy said? Something about Quentin not being a model housekeeper?

That, thought Marcia, was the understatement of the year.

Clothes were flung over the furniture, books, newspapers and dirty dishes were strewn on the tables and the floor and an easel and a clutter of painting equipment decorated the corner with the most light. She wrinkled her nose. Over the smell of turpentine and linseed oil was a nastier smell. From the kitchen. Bracing herself, she stepped over an untidy heap of art magazines and discovered on the counter the remains of Quentin's supper: a wilting Caesar salad over which three houseflies were circling. The anchovies were the source of the odor.

He might be a great artist. He was also a slob. By the look of it she wasn't going to get to her novels today; she was quite sure that she couldn't live with this mess.

Marcia went outside again, brought in all her stuff, then changed into a pair of shorts and a T-shirt and got to work.

The contents of the refrigerator revealed that Quentin liked foreign beer, Gruyère cheese and steak, but his taste in books was eclectic; several of them she herself was interested in reading. His clothes ran to the frankly shabby—a long way from the expensive suit he had worn at the opening.

In the back porch she found a pair of jeans and a shirt that were liberally daubed with mud; she dumped them in the washing machine in the basement, then, astounded that it was already midafternoon, made herself a cup of tea and a sandwich.

She'd run the vacuum over the floor when she'd finished, and shake the woven rugs outdoors. Then the downstairs would be done.

Because she was sitting down, she took the time to look around her. The house was constructed on an open plan, with thick beams supporting the high ceilings. Sunlight patterned the polished hardwoods floors and from every window Marcia could see trees and water and sky. Now that it was tidier, she could allow the spirit of the house to move her. A generous spirit, she thought. User-friendly.

One of Quentin's abstracts hung over the stone fireplace, its misty greens and blues pulling the outdoors within. She wasn't just tidying the house because mess offended her, she admitted to herself as she crunched on a raw carrot stick. She was tidying it to remove as many traces of Quentin as she could. Folding his clothes, washing dishes he had used, going through the pockets of his jeans before she put them in the washer—those had seemed very intimate acts. She knew a lot more about him than she had three hours ago. More than she wanted to know.

One thing was sure. If there were genes for cleanliness and neatness, Quentin certainly hadn't inherited his mother's.

The only things she hadn't tidied were Quentin's art supplies; somehow they seemed sacrosanct. Nor had she spent a lot of time looking at the painting on the easel, whose seething mass of sage-green coils, for all their interconnections, emitted a profound sense of disconnection. It was a disturbing painting. That it might have something to do with the way Quentin felt about her was more than she could deal with.

Half an hour later she finished the downstairs. With considerable satisfaction she looked around. Books and magazines shelved, a couple of her own books on the teak coffee-table and not a whiff of anchovy. Determinedly she headed up the stairs. But she found herself hesitating in the doorway of the master bedroom, and it was with palpable reluctance that she entered.

The first thing she saw was the unmade bed. Her mouth dry, she let her eyes flicker round the room—a beautifully proportioned room with nooks filled with cushions and skylights in the angled ceiling. The walls were a soft off-white between cedar-stained beams.

The painting over the bed made her smile, reminding her of the one Troy had bought for her. A small boy was fishing in a river, the peace of the scene enfolding her almost physically. But as she went to strip the bed a second painting struck her like an ambush: an abstract that was like a cry of pain. She backed away from it, remembering the torment in Quentin's face the last time she had seen him.

She'd done the right thing. She *had*.

Her jaw set, ignoring the indentation in the pillow where Quentin's head had lain, she yanked the sheets from the bed and added them to the pile of washing. There was no sign of any pajamas.

Maybe he slept naked.

Oh, stop it, Marcia! You've done nothing but think about Quentin ever since you arrived. How he sleeps—with whom he sleeps—is nothing to do with you. You rejected him, right?

Had Lucy suggested the stay here knowing that Marcia wouldn't be able to escape the presence of a man whose magnetism and talent infused every room of the house?

I could go home, Marcia thought, taking clean sheets out of the linen cupboard. But I don't want to. For one thing, that would be admitting defeat. Quentin would have won were she to get in her car and drive back to her condo.

Once she'd finished cleaning up she'd forget about him. She could always hide the paintings under the bed while she was here.

The other reason she didn't want to go home was a dim intuition that she needed a few days away from all her normal concerns. From her condo and her job and her family. Maybe then she'd be able to figure out what was going on. Why she loved and envied Lucy. Why she worked all the time.

Why a blue-eyed man was haunting her dreams.

CHAPTER FOUR

WHEN she went for a walk before supper Marcia discovered a screened-in gazebo by the edge of the lake, with a hammock strung from its beams. For a whole hour she lay in it, her book open on her chest, the ripple of the water lulling her into a kind of peace she rarely allowed herself to experience. She then went back to the house, turned on some music and made spinach linguine with a clam sauce followed by a fruit salad. She topped off this exceedingly healthy meal with a chocolate-coated marzipan bar from her favorite German bakery. Then she got up to change the tape.

The sun was setting behind the trees, whose shadows lay like bars across the grass. The birds were no longer singing. When she pushed the eject button on the tape player, the noise was shockingly loud.

She felt a shiver of unease. There was not another house in sight, and it had never occurred to her to drive further along the road to see where her nearest neighbors lived. She went into the kitchen and checked that the back door was locked, pulling the blind down over the window. Then she closed and bolted all the downstairs windows. She washed and dried the dishes. She put on more music and opened her novel.

It was a slick and cleverly written book that totally failed to hold her interest. She made a batch of fudge bars and washed more dishes, and then wished that she hadn't cleaned the house so thoroughly earlier in the day so she could do it now, or that she'd brought some of her notes from the lab to work on. It was completely

dark outside, in a way the city never was dark. To prove
something to herself, Marcia went out on the stone step.
The sky was spangled with stars, cold pinpricks of light
that spoke of immense distance and her own insignifi-
cance. Of her own loneliness.

Everyone gets lonely, she thought irritably, and went
back indoors, where she picked out a different book and
forced herself to read until ten-thirty. Then she had a
shower, put on silk mandarin pajamas and went into the
bedroom.

Not stopping to think, she took down the abstract
painting, wrapped it in her other pair of silk pajamas
and tucked it between the bureau and the wall. Standing
on the mattress, she opened the skylight, because the
sun had warmed the room and she was sure it wasn't
going to rain. Finally she flipped off the bedside lamp
and lay down on the bed. The bed Quentin had slept in
only two nights ago.

She wasn't going to think about Quentin. She was
going to sleep.

Which, almost instantly, she did.

Marcia woke to pitch darkness. Rubbing her eyes, she
pulled the blankets to her chin because she was cold.
The red numbers on the digital clock informed her that
it was ten to one. And then she heard the sound that
must have woken her, and sat bolt-upright.

The slam of a car door. Outside the house.

She'd been right to be afraid of her isolation, and cri-
minally foolish not to have looked up her nearest
neighbors. Who was it? A burglar? A vandal? One thing
was sure: she wasn't going to stay around to find out.

Moving as quietly as she could, Marcia opened the
skylight as far as it would go. Then she bent her knees
and pushed off from the bed with as much of a leap as
she could manage, hitching herself over the lower edge

of the window. The wooden rim dug into her ribs. With a strength born of fear she wriggled through the opening and rolled over onto the roof. Then she lay very still, her thighs and belly pressed into the slats, her ears straining to hear what was happening.

A light flipped on downstairs, throwing gold rectangles on the grass. The darkness had been protection of a kind and Marcia closed her eyes tight shut, understanding perfectly well why ostriches hid their heads in the sand. Then every muscle tensed and her eyes flew open again as below her someone walked into the bedroom. More light, flooding out onto the roof, making her feel exposed and helpless. She held her breath. To her relief she heard a diminishing thud of footsteps on the stairs, followed by silence.

Marcia dug her toes into the roof to keep from sliding downwards, wondering how long she'd be able to maintain her position. Gravity, she thought with a ridiculous urge to giggle, was already beginning to win out. She shouldn't have eaten that last fudge bar.

From somewhere downstairs a voice called her name. A man's voice. "Marcia! Where in God's name are you? It's me, Quentin. You don't need to be afraid...Marcia?"

Quentin. Here at the cottage. Not an unknown burglar. Her pent-up breath swooshed out of her lungs and her hold relaxed. With a yelp of terror she felt herself slide downward. Grabbing for the edge of the skylight, Marcia held on tight.

She heard feet taking the stairs two at a time. Then the floorboards creaked in the bedroom. "Marcia? Where—?" A face thrust itself in the gap between the window and the roof and a pair of very blue eyes looked right at her. "God almighty, woman," Quentin said, "you scared the living daylights out of me."

"*I* scared *you*?" she croaked. "What do you think you did to me?"

"What in hell are you doing out on the roof?"

He looked solid and real and reassuringly familiar. Light-headed with relief, Marcia said, "Star-gazing? Owl-watching? What do you think I'm doing on the roof? I'm hiding from the burglar-cum-rapist-cum-murderer who was about to burst into my bedroom."

"It's not your bedroom. It's mine."

"Don't be so picky about the details," she said fractiously.

The turmoil of fear in Quentin's chest began to subside, to be replaced by an equally tumultuous joy. Marcia was here. Here at the cottage. He had no idea why and he didn't really care. Enough that he was with her. Her eyes were black as the sky and her hair framed cheekbones that he itched to draw and lips that he longed to kiss. He said, his eyes glinting, "You look beauteous as the night—I think I should serenade you."

Marcia's arms were aching. But she seemed to have left behind her sensible, workaday self when she'd scrambled up on the roof. "I've never been serenaded on a rooftop before."

The emotion he felt was unquestionably jealousy. "And where *have* you been serenaded, Marcia Barnes?"

She wrinkled her nose. "I was serenaded on a very dirty canal in Venice by a gondolier who charged plenty for the privilege. That's not very romantic, is it?"

"Surely I can better that," said Quentin. "Are the men in Ottawa such wimps that they run for cover when you look down your pretty little nose at them?"

"Men are rats," Marcia said vigorously.

"And how many men are you basing that conclusion on?" Quentin demanded, his imagination presenting him with a line-up of men stretching from the Byward Market all the way to the Houses of Parliament.

"Quentin, I am not going to discuss my love-life when I'm hanging by the fingernails over a fifteen-foot drop."

"You've got a point. Here, grab hold of me and we'll get you back into the room."

She wrapped her fingers around his wrist and tried to push herself back through the gap. A shingle scraped her anklebone, and her left elbow and the window frame connected with bruising force. Then somehow she was sliding through the window, faster and faster, her face jammed into Quentin's chest. He staggered backward and the two of them landed in a tangled heap on the bed.

Marcia was mostly underneath. He was wearing a cotton shirt through which she could feel the curve of his collarbone and the warmth of his skin; his shoulder was crushing her breast and his thighs had her pinned to the mattress. He was heavy. But not so heavy that she wanted him to move.

Then he did move, levering himself up on one elbow. "Are you all right?" he said urgently.

There was a fan of tiny lines at each corner of his eyes. His hair had tumbled over his forehead. It's a good thing my arms aren't free, thought Marcia in mingled panic and desire. Because if they were, I'd be pulling you down to kiss me, Quentin Ramsey, and to heck with the consequences.

Perhaps her impulse had shown in her face. He said roughly, "If someone'd told me when I got up this morning that I'd end up the day in bed with you, Marcia, I'd have told them they were clean out of their mind."

"We're not in—"

"Oh, yes, we are." He adjusted his wrist to make her more comfortable, letting his gaze run over her flushed cheeks, the jut of her breasts under the pale gray silk, the fragile bones of her wrist. "I think we should take advantage of it, don't you?"

He was lowering his head to kiss her, and any protest she might have made died. Mesmerized, she closed her eyes, and felt the first warm pressure of his mouth on hers. Warm, unexpectedly gentle, and with a leisurely sensuality that made her head swim. He brushed her lips with his as lightly as the touch of a feather; he nibbled on her lower lip and stroked her cheek, sliding his mouth over her cheekbone to her ear, pushing back her hair with his fingers. And all the while she was achingly aware of the weight and heat of his body hard against her.

With a tentative shyness that told a great deal about her, Marcia reached up her hands to touch his face. As she buried them in his wiry black curls, digging into his scalp, he murmured with pleasure. The nape of his neck was taut, blending into the muscled breadth of his shoulders.

His shirt felt unnatural, like a barrier, and perhaps it was this that brought Marcia to an awareness of the melting heat of her own limbs and the ache of desire deep in her belly. She moved beneath him, and with a shock that raced through her frame felt the hardness of his erection between her legs. Not for the world could she have prevented her indrawn breath, her small, involuntary sound of yearning.

"Marcia..." he whispered, and found her mouth again, deepening his kiss, parting her lips to the thrust of his tongue.

It was her dream, she thought in confusion. She was drowning in the blue depths of a man's eyes. A man who was virtually a stranger to her. She twisted her head free and gasped, "Quentin, please...we mustn't."

His body was nothing but need, a fierce, impelling need to empty himself within this woman who was his completion in ways he didn't even understand. Blindly he sought for her lips again. But she pushed him away, her face distraught and her eyes full of frantic pleading. Like a man emerging from a dream, Quentin said hoarsely, "Did I hurt you? I didn't mean—"

"No. No, you didn't. But we've got to stop."

He stroked her hair back from her face, his fingers trembling very slightly. "Why?" he asked. "Nothing I've ever done in my entire life has felt more right than being here with you."

Marcia gaped up at him. "How can you say that? You don't even know me."

"I think I've always known you."

If any other man had said that to her, she would have laughed in his face. But somehow she knew that Quentin wasn't joking. "I'll say one thing to you," she said warmly, "your approach is unique."

His gaze inimical, he rasped, "You figure I'm stringing you a line so we'll really end up in bed?"

"If this is just the dress rehearsal, the performance must be beyond belief," Marcia said recklessly, and with a surge of exhilaration knew she had spoken the exact truth.

"Oh, it will be . . . trust me," he said, moving his hand very lightly across the patterned silk of her top until it lay on her breast, his palm cupping the small, firm swell of her flesh. He felt her shiver with pleasure, her nipple tightening, and said with fierce impatience, "Let's make love, Marcia. Now. Maybe that's the way you and I should get to know one another—with our bodies. Leaving out all the social chitchat because we know what matters."

He teased her nipple in his fingers, watching her eyes darken with desire. "The two of us in bed together. That's what matters," he went on with passionate intensity. "Pleasing each other. Loving each other. We can catch up on the other stuff later; we'll have all kinds of time for that. But right now I want you so badly I can't think straight."

Against her ribcage she could feel the heavy pounding of his heart; at the open neck of his shirt, like an echo, was the rapid beat of his pulse. Knowing his honesty deserved a matching honesty from her, Marcia said, "I'm too scared, Quentin."

"I wouldn't hurt you for the world."

"It's myself I'm scared of, not you. I never behave like this—never!"

He brought her hand to his mouth, sucking very gently on each of her fingertips in turn. "How don't you behave? Show me."

His mouth was slick and wet on her skin, making nonsense of shyness or resistance. Impulsively Marcia did exactly what she wanted to do. She circled her hips beneath him, slowly and suggestively, rubbing against the hardness that was the outward mark of his hunger. Then she pulled his head down, kissing him with a wanton passion she hadn't known she was capable of. He groaned her name deep in his throat and rolled over, his hand roaming the long curve of her spine as he pulled her on top of him. Her ankle struck his shin; she flinched with pain.

"What's wrong?" Quentin sat up, his arm around her. "Your ankle—Marcia, you're bleeding."

"I must have done it on the roof," she mumbled. "The shingles are made of wood and the edges are sharp."

She didn't want to talk about roofs and shingles. She wanted to be at the center of a desire so all-consuming that she didn't have to think, didn't have to be cautious and controlling and careful. A desire that obliterated the Marcia she'd always been. She reached out her hand to take him by the shoulder.

But Quentin didn't even see her small gesture. He slid off the bed. "Stay put—I'll be right back."

Marcia's hand fell back on the bed and she stayed where she was, mostly because she didn't think she could stand up. The air coming through the skylight was cool; chills rippled across her skin. She felt—she sought for

the word to express the yawning emptiness within her—
bereft. That was it. Bereft.

Quentin came back in the room, carrying a towel, a
small bowl of water and a first-aid kit. "I hope you didn't
get any splinters in it."

She glanced down. "I don't think so. Don't fuss,
Quentin, it's really nothing."

"I know you're the doctor—but let me do this, all
right?"

"All right," said Marcia, with a meekness that would
have astonished Lucy. She had bled on the sheets.
Another load for the washer.

Quentin lifted her foot and put the towel under it,
then carefully began to wash the blood from the two-
inch scrape. He could easily have circled her ankle in his
fingers; her skin was smooth, the veins blue in the high
arch of her foot. He dabbed away at the flecks of dirt
at the edges of the scrape, trying to concentrate on his
task. Then he spread on an antibiotic cream, added a
gauze pad and bandage, and taped it in place.

Despite himself, his hand lingered, tracing the slender
bones on top of her foot. Although her pajamas had a
high collar, long sleeves and slim trousers that came to
mid-calf, the silk fabric tended to cling, revealing as well
as concealing; he remembered how her breast had nestled
in his hand like a bird and said overloudly, "The prog-
nosis is good. The patient will survive."

But Marcia didn't laugh. Instead he saw that tears were
shimmering in her eyes. Swiftly he rested his hand on
her knee. "Did I hurt you?"

She shook her head. "I—I guess I'm not used to being
looked after, that's all."

"You don't let people look after you."

Her chin tilted in a way he was beginning to re-
cognize. "I like being independent."

"Ain't that the truth?"

"There's nothing wrong with being independent! I like making my own decisions and having my own money and—"

"Marcia, we are not going to argue about independence at two o'clock in the morning. Lie down and I'll get you an extra blanket. You look cold."

She was cold, inside as well as out. "But this is your room," she faltered.

"I'll sleep in the spare room." He took a fleecy blanket out of the closet. She was still sitting up in the middle of the bed, clutching the sheets to her chin, her eyes huge; he had no idea what she was thinking. He was a damned fool to be giving her a blanket when there were other, much more enjoyable ways of keeping her warm, but while her kisses had nearly driven him out of his mind, some deep instinct was warning him not to push his luck. To have found her here at the cottage was a miracle. Don't rush her, Quentin, he told himself. She'll still be here in the morning. And she's worth waiting for.

She's the one you've been waiting for all your life.

"Lie down," he said, "you look tired out."

Didn't he want her any more? Was that what he was saying? Obediently Marcia lay down, watching him draw the covers over her. "Goodnight," she whispered.

Briefly his lips were warm on her cheek. "Sleep well," he said. Then he padded out of the room, switching out the light and leaving her alone in the darkness.

I don't know who I am any more, thought Marcia. I would have made love with a man I don't even know. A man who terrifies the life out of me. I wanted to tear the clothes from his body. Me, Marcia Barnes. What's happening to me? I've got to get out of here before I do something I'll regret.

She closed her eyes, snuggling into the warmth of the blankets, already planning how she would leave before breakfast. She was mentally removing her food from the refrigerator when, as if a thick, black blanket had been thrown over all the others, she fell fast asleep.

CHAPTER FIVE

MARCIA woke to hear a robin caroling lustily in the trees over her head. The sky was a brilliant blue. The clock beside the bed said ten-thirty.

She'd meant to wake up early. So she could sneak out before Quentin woke up.

As she stretched, feeling various aches and pains make themselves known from her precipitate ascent to the roof and just as precipitate descent from it, her thoughts marched on. She'd felt safe falling asleep in the middle of the night, knowing that Quentin was sharing the house with her; she didn't like being all alone in the woods, she'd found that out yesterday evening. She still felt safe this morning. How could she feel safe and unsafe with one and the same man? It didn't make sense.

The trilliums in the woods were beautiful. And in the gazebo she'd actually managed to relax for a whole hour. A new record, she thought ruefully. No wonder part of me doesn't want to leave here this morning. After all, if Quentin hadn't arrived in the middle of the night I wouldn't have woken up. I'd have been all right here on my own. Not totally comfortable. But all right.

I don't want to spend the rest of the week in my condo.

Damn him anyway! Why hadn't he stayed in New York?

If only he'd stayed in New York, she would still have been ignorant of the new Marcia who had emerged last night in this very bed. As she remembered the way she'd writhed beneath him, kissing him with such abandon, shame warmed her cheeks. How *could* she have behaved like that? It was totally out of character. The sooner she got home and forgot about that new Marcia, the better.

She got out of bed, limping a little on her sore ankle, and dressed in a long-sleeved shirt that hid her bruised elbow and cotton trousers that covered Quentin's bandage; she shoved her glasses on her nose, then she folded and packed her clothes into her suitcase and headed for the bathroom. Ten minutes later, her make-up impeccable, her hair smoothly shining, she went downstairs carrying her bag.

Quentin was nowhere to be seen. Quickly she opened the refrigerator and repacked her cooler, then bundled the other food she'd brought into plastic bags. She was gathering her books when through the big windows she caught sight of something moving in the woods. She straightened, holding the books, her throat suddenly dry.

Quentin had been swimming in the lake. He was striding toward the house, a towel flung over one shoulder, his swim trunks sitting low on his hips. Patterns of sun and shadow moved over the muscled planes of his body. He had a beautiful body, she thought unwillingly, deep-chested, lean-hipped, consummately male. But more than that he looked happy, as happy and carefree as a boy, and as much a part of his surroundings as the house was.

It was a good thing she was going. Quentin Ramsey spelled trouble with a capital T.

He came in the door and grinned at her. "Pour me a cup of coffee, woman. The water's freezing and—" His eyes narrowed as he suddenly saw her belongings neatly arrayed on the floor. "What the devil are you doing?"

Drops of water were trickling down his shoulders to be caught in the dark hair on his chest. Marcia dragged her eyes away and said with as much dignity as she could muster, "I'm leaving."

"*Leaving*? What for?"

"The reason's very simple—you came back from New York."

He planted himself in front of the door and began scrubbing at his chest with the towel. "I couldn't stand it there," he said. "Hot, dirty, and too many people. I did what needed to be done at the gallery and caught the night flight home. Tell me the real reason why you can't stay."

She clamped down on her temper. "I've already told you—because you're here."

"What's so awful about me?"

What's awful is the way I behave around you... But Marcia said, spacing her words as if she were explaining something to a small and not overly bright child, "I came here on the understanding that you'd be away until Friday. You came back. I, therefore, am leaving."

"This is Tuesday. Why aren't you at work?"

"Budget cuts," she snapped. "Unpaid leave."

"Well, hurray for the government. Best thing they've done for me all year. Don't you like the house?"

"I love the house."

"The woods, the lake—not to your taste?"

"Quentin, quit playing games! We both know what could have happened last night. I—"

"What if it had? Would that have been so terrible?"

"Of course it would. I'm not into casual sex."

"Neither am I," he said softly.

Marcia flushed scarlet. Breathing hard, she seethed, "Then I would have thought you'd be pushing me out the door."

"The way I feel about you is not casual," Quentin said. "Haven't you gotten that message yet?"

"The only message I've been getting is that all your other females have been willing."

"For Pete's sake—you make it sound as though I keep a harem!"

"I saw how those women clustered round you at the gallery—and you weren't exactly discouraging them."

"Jealous, Marcia?"

"Of course not."

"I don't believe you."

"Are you calling me a liar?" she snapped.

"Let me set the record straight. One, I'm not Don Juan. Two, I've already told you you're special to me in ways I don't understand. Three, if we'd made love last night I'd have done my best to give you pleasure, to make you feel desirable and wanted and fulfilled. Because that way I—"

With unconscious drama Marcia covered her ears with her hands. "Stop!" she choked. "I scarcely know you. How can I possibly go to bed with you?"

"How about because you want to?"

She dropped her hands, recalled in graphic detail how she had kissed him, and to her horror burst into tears. Weeping as though her heart would break, she fell backward onto the chesterfield and shoved her head into the crook of her elbow.

Appalled, Quentin let the towel fall to the floor and knelt beside her, raising her head to remove her glasses then pressing her face into his bare shoulder. His body was shuddering with the intensity of her feelings, and in between noisy sobs that seemed to tear their way out of her chest he heard her wail, "I never cry. N-never. I hate c-crying."

"Never" seemed to be Marcia's favorite word. Quentin murmured nonsensical words of comfort into her ear and wondered if he'd ever felt this way about a woman before. He was pretty sure that he hadn't, because he couldn't imagine forgetting it if he had. Tenderness, exasperation, the longing to console, all mixed together with a healthy dose of good old-fashioned lust. Her hair smelled sweet. The narrowness of her shoulders both excited and frightened him, filling him with the need to protect her. Lust he knew. But tenderness? Protection?

Love?

He found himself shying away from the word. To love a woman would change his life drastically—particularly if the woman in question wasn't into being loved. *Was* Marcia the right woman? How could he answer that? It would take, he realized for the first time, two people to answer that question. He'd never realized that before.

Not liking the direction his thoughts were taking, he said, "Guess what, Marcia? I don't have a handkerchief."

His voice seemed to come from a long way away; she felt as though she'd been run over by a truck. Her breath heaving in her throat, Marcia mumbled, "I've got a tissue in my pocket."

Where Quentin's shoulder had been wet with lake-water, it was now wet with tears. She sat up, avoiding his eyes, and blew her nose with gusto. Then she hiccuped, "I hate women who c-cry. It's so feminine. Such an underhanded way t-to win an argument."

"Who said you'd won?"

She glowered at him, her nose and eyes pink, her lashes sticking together in little clumps that filled him with an even deeper tenderness than before. "Quentin, I'm leaving."

"Over my dead body, sweetie."

With a flash of humor that heartened him immensely, she retorted, "The woman I've always been may be falling apart around me, but I d-don't really think I'm cut out to be a murderess."

"Good." He grinned at her, sitting down on the chesterfield beside her. "You're staying. Right here where you belong."

"Oh, yeah? That's what you think." Which was, she thought with another reprehensible quiver of amusement, a reply worthy of the playground, not of a woman who could put half a dozen letters after her name.

"The Richardsons are away all month, and I'm keeping an eye on the house for them—so I can invite whoever I want to stay here. You're it."

"Keeping an eye on the house? Huh. The place was a pigsty." Marcia scrubbed at her wet cheeks with the back of her hand and put her glasses back on. "Actually, that's an insult to pigs."

"When I first walked in last night I thought I was in the wrong house," Quentin admitted meekly. "All that tidiness. It's because I was working on a painting, Marcia—I'm always messy when I paint. The rest of the time I'm really quite civilized."

Of all the adjectives she might have applied to Quentin, "civilized" wouldn't have topped the list. Frowning, she tried to behave like a sensible, rational adult. "I don't understand why you want me to stay."

"I'll tell you why if you'll tell me why you were crying."

"That's private!"

"You've been private all your life," Quentin said ruthlessly, "and it's not working, is it?"

"I hate it when you talk about me to Lucy."

"Anything you tell me stops right here."

The odd thing was that she believed him instantly. And after all, hadn't she come here to try and figure herself out? "All right," Marcia said ungraciously.

Quentin hadn't expected her to surrender quite so easily. Choosing his words, he said, "When I arrived here last night and found a strange car in the driveway and the living room looking like a photo in a glossy magazine, I didn't know what was going on. Then I picked up a book on the table and saw your name in it. I wasn't just happy, Marcia—too mild a word by far.

Joy. That's what I felt. Joy... And explain that to me if you can.''

He ran his fingers through his wet hair. ''I'd already been through the house and I knew it was empty. So where were you? In the space of two seconds I had you dead, lost, raped, murdered, drowned—you name it. When I found you on the roof I wanted to hold onto you and never let you go.''

He got up, prowling restlessly round the room. ''You're important to me—I've told you that before and last night only confirmed it.'' Scowling at the easel, he added, ''You must have looked at that... it's how I've been feeling ever since the dinner at your place, when you told me you didn't want to see me again. Stay, Marcia—please.''

So her suspicion that the painting was related to her had been quite correct. ''You sure say it how it is,'' she said quietly.

''I can't be bothered with all the shenanigans people go through. Take a look at a wildflower sometime—or a lake in the sunlight. What's manipulation got to do with that?''

Marcia remembered the dappled sunlight on the carpet of trilliums and knew that he was right. Unable to think of anything to say, she stared down at her fingers, which were nervously twining and intertwining in her lap.

Quentin wiped the towel over the back of his neck, where water was still dribbling from his hair. Kissing her would convince her of the strength of his feelings, but he was almost sure she'd belt him if he were to try that particular argument. ''I want you to stay for your sake as well as mine,'' he said.

With none of her usual grace Marcia got to her feet, putting the chesterfield like a barrier between her and the man pacing up and down the hardwood floor. He'd finished. It was her turn now. But what was she going to say?

"I've always been in control of my life and my emotions—of everything," she faltered. "But lately... I don't know what's happening—and it's not just you. I *never* cry. Three times in a row in that damned gallery I could have bawled my eyes out." She dug her nails into the padded fabric and added in a rush, "I really hate this—I hate talking about myself."

Smothering the urge to take her in his arms, Quentin said gently, "You're doing just fine."

"Sex," she blurted. "That's why I cried."

His whole body tensed. "What do you mean?"

She gulped, "I'm ashamed to even think how I behaved last night."

"Marcia—"

"I suppose it's understandable if I analyze it. I was frightened when I heard someone in the house, then I spent a very uncomfortable few minutes on the roof and then you literally fell on me. Little wonder I behaved so abnormally."

His voice was as sharp as a knife-blade. "Do you really believe that?"

"I'm not sexy like Lucy," she said desperately.

Feeling his way, Quentin replied, "Of course you're not. You're sexy like Marcia."

"But you'd much rather I was like Lucy."

He hesitated fractionally, remembering his first sight of Marcia, so perfectly groomed in her severe tailored suit, her glasses warding off the world—just as they were now. His disappointment had been acute; he remembered that too.

Marcia paled. "You're in love with Lucy."

"For God's sake—"

"You'd have to be! I know you spent a lot of time with her on the island that summer she and Troy were separated, and she's so beautiful, and all her emotions spill all over the place—you'd have to be a chunk of rock not to fall in love with her."

"Marcia," Quentin said forcefully, "I never was the slightest bit in love with Lucy."

"She's got a gorgeous figure," Marcia wailed, "I can see— *What* did you say?"

"I never for one instant was in love with Lucy. When she turned up on Shag Island looking as miserable as a stray cat she was like the sister I never had. I couldn't have been happier when she and Troy got back together, and since then they've become two of my closest friends."

"Oh," said Marcia.

Wondering if he was burning all his bridges behind him, Quentin said, "Lucy's beautiful; sure she is. But she never once touched my soul. And I certainly never wanted to take her to bed. Not like you."

"But—"

He sat down on the arm of the nearest chair, smiling at her. "Your pajamas—let alone what you're wearing now—could have been worn by any self-respecting nun, and I was still half crazy with desire. I hate to think what'll happen when I see you in a pair of shorts."

She said in a small voice, "I've envied Lucy for years— I'm just beginning to realize that. She was always in love with someone, she always did what she wanted, even when the rest of the family didn't approve, and she was the only one of us who didn't become a doctor—she seemed so free."

"Lucy's one of the lucky ones, who was born knowing what she wanted, and had the confidence to go after it. It's just taken you longer, that's all." He put all the force of his personality behind his words. "You did nothing to be ashamed of last night, Marcia. That woman is the woman you're meant to be."

"I'm not in love with you," she flashed.

He didn't like her saying that. Didn't like it at all. He said shortly, "It's too soon to talk about love."

"But you want to make love with me. Or so you say."

Her knuckles were white where she was gripping the back of the chesterfield. She was like a wild creature, Quentin thought, who was trapped in a corner and lashing out at anyone who came too close. "If you'll stay for a few days, I won't so much as touch you," he said. "I swear I won't."

And how in heaven's name was he going to manage that?

Some of the tension left her shoulders. "Not even if I wear my shorts?" she said with a tiny smile.

"Right," he said ironically. "Will you stay?"

A question made up of three small words on which her whole life seemed to depend. "Yes...I guess so."

He felt suddenly exhausted, as though he'd swum the whole length of the lake. "Good," he said. "Why don't you unpack and I'll make you some breakfast?"

"We should change bedrooms."

He raised his brow. "You'd better stay in that room— I wouldn't want to deprive you of your escape route. I'll go up and get dressed...back in a minute."

So Marcia spent the next ten minutes putting her food back in the cupboards and the refrigerator and wondering if she was being a total idiot to stay in the same house with Quentin.

Two days later Marcia was no nearer a conclusion. Quentin was keeping scrupulously to his bargain—so scrupulously that she wondered sometimes if she'd dreamed him saying how much he wanted her. She'd worn her shorts yesterday, and so far as she could tell he hadn't given her legs—which she'd always thought rather shapely—so much as a passing glance. He was giving her lots of space—swimming at least twice a day in water so cold it made her shudder, and disappearing on long walks through the woods; he appeared to have abandoned his painting.

At mealtimes he barbecued steak and chicken while she made pasta and salads, and they each made conversation that left her feeling utterly frustrated in a way she couldn't pinpoint. The most significant thing she'd learned about him was that eating shrimp made him violently ill. It didn't seem like much for two whole days. Not from a man who kept saying she was important to him.

It was as though the real man had gone somewhere else, leaving a pleasant, considerate, distant stranger.

She tried her best to relax. She took books to the gazebo and lay in the hammock and all the time she was wondering what Quentin was doing. When he settled down with a book in the house she'd meander along the lakeshore by herself, her nerves on edge in a way she deplored but couldn't prevent. Wondering if busyness could be the antidote, she vacuumed, made cookies, raked the lawn and weeded around the shrubs. She went to bed early and got up late.

Nothing helped. Every moment of the day, or so it seemed to her, she was achingly aware of the man who was sharing the house with her. He was keeping to his promise. Why, then, was she so angry with him?

On Thursday afternoon Quentin was hunched over some drawings at the dining room table, and something in the line of his back told Marcia not to disturb him. She went outside, slathering fly dope on her arms and legs, and set off down the shore. In a little cove ten minutes from the house she sat down on a rock, staring glumly at the water. The only thing she'd accomplished this week was not missing the lab. She'd been too busy missing Quentin.

How could she miss someone she was virtually living with?

Through a gap in the rocks a muskrat headed purposefully for the grasses along the shore. Marcia sat as still as a rock herself, watching in fascination as it nibbled at the fresh shoots, its wet fur gleaming in the sun. Then a second animal appeared round the corner, heading for the same cluster of rushes; the first one chattered and gibbered at it in clear displeasure, then plunged after it, its long tail whipping like a snake in the water. Both of them vanished from the cove. Little ripples spread across the water and splashed against the rocks.

Grinning to herself, Marcia stood up and hurried back to the house. Quentin was bent over the table. She said, "Guess what? I saw two muskrats."

"Yeah?" he said, not looking up.

She marched across the room and stood right in front of him. "Quentin, I'm speaking to you."

"Just a sec."

In a glorious flood of energy Marcia lost her temper. "I can't imagine why you were so insistent I stay here," she blazed. "You pay me less attention than if I were a slab of sirloin steak, and if this is how you behave when someone touches your soul, I'd sure hate to be around you if you were indifferent to me."

He pushed back his chair. "What the hell's gotten into you?"

"I absolutely loathe being treated like a stick of furniture!"

Her hands were on her hips, her shorts were several inches briefer than the ones she'd worn yesterday, and her violet eyes were flashing like amethysts. "That was the deal we made," Quentin snarled. "That I wouldn't touch you."

Her nostrils flared. "I didn't think we made a deal that you'd totally ignore my existence."

"It's pretty hard to do that when every time I turn around you're dusting and cleaning and tidying up."

"If you weren't so messy, I wouldn't have to!"

"You know what your problem is? You don't know the meaning of the word vacation!"

He knew exactly where to put the knife so it would hurt most. "I wish you'd never come back from New York," she said viciously.

"Not half as much as I do."

Marcia's temper vanished as precipitously as it had arisen. A cold knot of fear in the pit of her stomach, she gasped, "Is that true?"

Quentin thrust his hands in his pockets. "No."

Trying very hard to mask her relief, she said petulantly, "You're a fine one to talk about vacations. Look at you—you never stop painting and drawing." Frowning in puzzlement, she stared at the strewn papers. "That looks like a house plan." She looked closer. "A house like this."

"That's precisely what it is," he said impatiently.

"If you want one like it, couldn't you get a copy of the plans from the builder?"

"Marcia, I was the builder."

She gaped at him. "You mean, you built this house?"

"I thought you knew that—didn't Lucy tell you?"

"She did not." She looked around at the angled ceilings and the shadowed beams with new eyes. "Did you design it as well?" When he nodded she said warmly, "It's a beautiful house. Where did you learn how to do that?"

Her whole face was alight with interest. Keeping his hands firmly in his pockets, Quentin said, "From my dad. I started drawing things as soon as I was old enough to hold a crayon, and it must have been clear to him that I was going to be an artist—especially after I did drawings of our seven chickens all over the kitchen wallpaper when I was five. He never discouraged me. In fact, he kind of liked it when I did sketches of the lumber crew that he could show off to his buddies. But the idea that I might earn my living as an artist—he didn't think too much of that. So he made sure I learned everything he knew about carpentry, so I'd have something real I could depend on."

There was a half-smile on his face and his eyes were soft; Quentin had loved his father, that much was obvious. Her own father had died when she was five, a long-ago pain Marcia had done her best to repress. "Did he build houses too?" she asked.

"Sheds and repairs to the camp, that's all. But the people my mother worked for had a timber-frame house built for them by some contractors from the States, and that's when I fell in love with that kind of construction. All the posts and beams exposed, and the wonderful sense of space."

"Quentin," Marcia said, "this is the first real conversation we've had in three days."

His smile was wry. "Yeah... I overestimated my ability to keep my hands off you."

"I thought you didn't want me anymore."

His laugh was unamused. "Oh, sure."

She said rapidly, before she could lose her nerve, "The reason I told you men were rats was because the only two men I've ever slept with both lied to me. Big time. And then you came along. First you said all that stuff about how I touched your soul and how I was so desirable and sexy—and then we made the deal that you wouldn't touch me and you stopped saying it. I figured it was a line you'd been feeding me to get me into bed. A line that hadn't worked, so you'd dropped it." She paused for breath. "You'd lied to me, in other words."

His eyes narrow. "Are you serious?"

"You know how I hate talking about myself. Of course I'm serious."

There was only one way he knew of to reassure her. In two quick strides Quentin closed the gap between them. He put his arms around Marcia and bent his head to kiss her, using all his considerable powers of imagination to show her with his mouth and his body how very much he wanted her. Almost immediately, intoxicated by the smooth curves of her bare arms, the swell of her hips and her flame-like response, he stopped thinking altogether.

Moments later they fell apart, staring at each other almost as if it was the first time they'd met. Quentin's chest was heaving as though he'd run all the way to the highway and back; Marcia's knees felt as insubstantial as the reeds that the muskrat had been eating. The muskrat that had started all this.

Quentin said jaggedly, "Let's take the car and go to the local store and get a couple of ice cream cones. Because if we don't, I'll be throwing you over my shoulder and making for the nearest bed."

"I only like vanilla," she whispered.

"Fussy, eh?"

"Very," she said, and smiled at him.

His heart turned over in his chest, for it was a smile from which she held nothing back, like a flower opening to the sun. "Marcia," he said huskily, "I—dammit, I don't even know what I want to say. I promise I won't lie to you—ever."

She thought of the painting of the three little girls running through the field, and for a moment she let her eyes wander around the generous and beautiful room in which she was standing. Swallowing hard, because she knew that she was taking a huge step, she said gravely, "I believe you."

"Trust...it's a big one, isn't it?"

"One of the biggest."

His smile crackling with energy, Quentin added, "If the local store doesn't have vanilla, we'll drive until we find one that does. Let's go."

He held out his hand. With a sense that she was doing something momentous Marcia took it, feeling his palm warm against hers. Together they went outside.

CHAPTER SIX

As HER footsteps crunched in the gravel driveway Marcia said, "We could take my car."

Quentin gave her battered gray vehicle a disparaging glance. "I thought doctors made lots of money."

Beside his bright yellow sports model, her car did look shabbier than usual. "Cars aren't important to me. I drive them until they fall apart and then I buy a new one."

"So what do you spend your money on?" he asked lightly.

She climbed into the passenger seat of his car, inhaling the scent of leather and admiring all the dials and gadgets. "Oh, the usual stuff," she said evasively. "Food, clothes, the mortgage."

"And that's it? No stocks and bonds? No rental properties?"

With a flash of spirit she said, "You're being very nosy."

"Aren't I just? Money has a lot of power in our society, so I'm always curious how people spend it."

Reaching into her handbag for her dark glasses, Marcia muttered, "Five years ago I went to India. I help support a village hospital in the north—near Delhi."

Quentin's hand froze on the clutch. "Ever since I went to Peru four years ago I've been supporting an orphanage there... The more I see of you, the more I realize that the very smooth front you present to the world is just that—a façade. Tell me about this hospital."

Not even Lucy and Troy knew about it. Slowly at first, but then with gathering enthusiasm, Marcia described the eye clinic and the preventive medicine unit—two of her pet projects. When she'd finished Quentin said soberly, "You're a good person, Marcia."

Feeling intensely shy, almost as though she'd taken off all her clothes in front of him, she said, "By the same token, so are you."

"A mutual admiration society?" He grinned at her and reversed in the driveway. "On a less lofty moral plane, you can now tell me about these two men. Whom I'm already prepared to thoroughly dislike."

"Do I have to?" she said, grimacing.

"Yep. And take your time. I want all the gory details. Start with number one. Name, age and occupation."

"It's going to be a triple ice cream cone," she said darkly. "With peanuts. Okay, okay, I'll start. Paul Epson. Third-year medical student. Twenty-one. I was eighteen, in my first year and away from home for the first time in my life. We fell in love and for six months I believed in every romantic cliché in the book.

"Then Paul started being less available and kind of distant...but I didn't really worry. He explained that his finals were getting close and he was under a lot of pressure. And I was buried under a mountain of work too. The whole thing fell apart when I met him at the frat house with another woman with whom he was quite clearly on intimate terms. He'd fallen out of love with me and into love with her, and the only thing he'd neglected to do was tell me."

Quentin said a word that made her blink. With more restraint he added, "Louse. Rat-fink. Yellow-bellied coward. Want me to go on?"

Marcia rather liked his response. "I was devastated. I wrote my finals in a daze, then I got the flu and couldn't shake it. I was working in a biochemistry lab for the summer, and I'd drag myself to work then go home and sleep for hours at a time, and get up just as tired as when I'd gone to bed—it was awful."

"What did your mother and Lucy think?"

"They didn't know anything about it! Mother wouldn't have approved of me sleeping with Paul and Lucy was always so busy." She cleared her throat, enjoying the breeze tugging at her hair as they drove along the country road. "Paul kind of discouraged me from trying again. And anyway, I was determined to make good marks and specialize. So I was twenty-five when I met man number two.

"Lester. Thirty-one, nephrologist, lived in Toronto. Very good-looking but kind of quiet and shy—or so I thought. We liked each other and we'd get together anytime I was in Toronto. Eventually he told me he was married but couldn't divorce his wife. She was in a mental institution—it was a very sad case, and I respected him for sticking with her. A few weeks later we became lovers."

She added with sudden fierceness, "It suited me, Quentin. Intimacy without involvement. Low-key. Discreet. And I've always been very wrapped up in my work—I didn't want a relationship that distracted me too much. We went on like that for four years. And then I went unexpectedly to a conference that he was attending. Guess what? He was there with his wife, who was no more a mental case than I am. A very wealthy wife. Whom of course he wouldn't divorce."

This time Quentin's epithet was unprintable. Marcia wrinkled her nose at him. "Thank you—but, you know, it served me right. He *was* a married man and I shouldn't have gotten involved with him. But how could he have deceived me so systematically for so long?" She sighed. "I came to the conclusion that I may be a very clever woman in the lab, but in the world of men I'm lacking the right radar."

Quentin was beginning to understand why she'd been keeping him at a distance. "Both of them went deep?" he ventured.

"Well, yes. I don't trust often, but when I do, it's total."

"I don't know how to convince you I'm different from them," he said slowly, braking and putting on the signal light. "Here's the store—maybe chocolate chip ice cream will help me think... Hey, what's going on?"

A woman was crouched near the wooden steps beside a little boy who was screaming at the top of his lungs—sharp screams of real pain. As Quentin parked the car Marcia leapt out and ran towards them. "I'm a doctor," she said, kneeling in the dirt driveway. "What happened?"

The mother, very young with copper curls, said frantically, "He fell off the steps."

Marcia smiled reassuringly at the boy and carefully probed his ankle. "He's sprained it—torn the ligament, by the feel of it." She looked over her shoulder. "Quentin, could you see if they have any ice in the store? It's okay, little guy, something cold will stop it hurting so much. What's your name?"

"Jason," said his mother. "He ran out ahead of me, and I tried to catch him but he fell before I could."

Quentin came down the steps, passing Marcia some ice cubes wrapped in his handkerchief. She put it round the swollen flesh. "There, Jason, that should help. Just give it a minute to kick in. You'll have to stay put for the next few days, I'm afraid." She smiled at his mother. "You'll probably want to call your regular doctor—you might need some painkillers for the rest of the day and tonight. But I really don't think anything's broken. Do you have a car?"

"Right over there."

Quentin said, "Here, I'll carry him."

Jason, who looked to be about four, had stopped screaming. "My popsicle's all dirty," he snuffled.

A bright red ice lolly was melting into the dirt; it was definitely not retrievable. Marcia said, "I'll go in and get you another one right now while my friend Quentin carries you to the car."

As she turned away she carried with her the image of Quentin gathering the little boy into his arms, his dark head bent, his big hands very gentle. One reason I envy Lucy is because she has Chris, she thought, with the jolt that an uncomfortable truth can bring with it. No wonder I've been avoiding her. All these years I've been fooling myself that I don't want children.

Did Quentin want them?

She hurried into the store and headed for the freezer. You're getting ahead of yourself, Marcia Barnes. You're terrified of going to bed with the man, and you're already thinking about children?

When she came back out Jason was strapped into the back seat of the car with his foot up. He accepted the popsicle with a wobbly grin, his mother thanked Marcia profusely and Marcia waved as they drove away. Quentin said thoughtfully, "You're good with kids."

"Ice cream, Quentin—we've earned it."

"I wouldn't mind having a couple of my own. Someday. What about you?" He added, "You're cute when you blush and even cuter when you're tongue-tied."

"It's a wonder to me that none of the women in your past has ever throttled you," Marcia said roundly, and realized that indirectly she was fishing for information.

"There haven't been that many, Marcia. I got married when I was twenty-five and Helen had divorced me by the time I was twenty-seven. For a very correct bank president twice her age with three times my salary. Living with an artist—so she told me—is only romantic when you're not doing it."

Marcia had never liked the name Helen. But to be jealous of a woman she'd never met was ridiculous. "She hurt you."

"We hurt each other. I should have listened to my intuition. When we were walking down the aisle together it was busy telling me I'd married the wrong woman because I'd been too impatient to wait for the right one." He raked his fingers through his hair. "Let's get that ice cream."

He'd been about to say something more, she would have sworn. She led the way up the steps and into the cool, cluttered interior of a store that sold everything from canned soup to garden shovels, stopping in front of the freezer with its cardboard containers of ice cream and aware through every nerve of Quentin coming up behind her. He drew her back against his body, wrapping his arms around her waist. "Vanilla and chocolate chip," he said. "We're in luck."

She leaned against him, loving the strength of his lean frame, curving her own arms over his and covering his hands with hers. He rubbed his cheek against her hair. "Have I told you yet today that you're gorgeous?"

She could feel the laughter in his chest. Leaning her weight on him, she closed her eyes in surrender, the words coming from somewhere deep within her. "Right this minute I feel superlatively happy."

His arms tightened their hold. "Oh, God, Marcia," he said helplessly, "you take my breath away. I'm different from Paul and Lester, I swear I am." He nuzzled his face into her neck, her soft skin and the sweet scent of her hair flooding his senses; against his arm he could feel her heartbeat quicken. "I am also," he added, "quite prepared to make love to you on top of the freezer."

"I know you are," she said wickedly. After a quick glance around to check that they were unobserved, she moved her hips from side to side with lazy sensuality.

"Stop it!" he said in a strangled voice.

"You started it," she replied with unarguable logic.

"We'd better buy a bushel of ice cream," he said, and released her.

She turned to face him, her eyes dancing. "I like you a lot better now than when you were being all tight-lipped and inscrutable."

"You think I did all that swimming in the lake for fun?" he rejoined, and watched her eyes widen and her cheeks grow pink.

"C'n I help you?"

The store's proprietor was a gnarled old man with eyes the shiny brown of chestnuts. "Two double cones, please," Marcia said, edging in front of Quentin. "One vanilla and one chocolate chip."

Quentin paid and they wandered outside, sitting at the picnic table near the river. Ice cream had never tasted so good, thought Marcia, entranced by the fresh green of the alders and by the reflections on the water, where blue shards of sky slid between moss-coated rocks. Everything seemed immediate, newly created. Was this how Quentin saw the world all the time? Was this how she could see it if she gave herself the time?

When he'd finished his cone, Quentin went back in the store and came out with a monstrous watermelon tucked under his arm. "I love it," he said defensively. "We could have a contest to see who can spit the seeds the furthest."

"And what's the prize?" she teased.

"A forfeit for the loser."

"I will not swim in the lake."

He leaned over and wiped a smear of ice cream from her lips. "That wasn't what I had in mind."

His blue eyes were intent on her face; he leaned closer and kissed her parted lips, the lightning flick of his tongue making her pulses race. "This contest could be dangerous," she said weakly. "For the winner and the loser."

"Let's go home," he said abruptly.

Home. A small word that struck her to her heart. "Where is your home, Quentin?" she asked. "Or do you still live in New Brunswick?"

It's wherever you are, he thought. "I haven't had a proper home for years," he said. "I've wandered all over the place—Asia, Africa, South America... although nearly every summer I go to Shag Island. I rent a little shack there. I've been wondering if the next house I build won't be my own. Somewhere on the west coast."

She, Marcia, worked in Ottawa. She said politely, "I'm sure it'll be lovely. Shall we go?"

Within ten minutes she was unlocking the front door of the house by the lake. She walked inside and it was as though the walls and the beams enclosed her, much as Quentin had enclosed her in his embrace. With no idea where the words came from she said, "What you do is so tangible. Paintings. Houses. You can see something for your work, touch it, look at it again and again, even live in it. Nothing I do is like that."

"Jason's mother wouldn't agree."

"Quentin, I spend my days in front of computer screens and gas chromatography units. I produce highly technical papers that only other immunologists will read. Oh, I know the research eventually reaches the public and makes a difference to people's health. But it's so indirect... and I don't know why the heck I'm saying this. I love my job. I always have. It's all I ever—"

She broke off as the telephone rang in the kitchen. Lifting his brows in surprise, Quentin went to answer it. "Hello... Hi, Lucy, how are you...? No, I came back early... She's still here, do you want to talk to her?" He held out the receiver. "It's Lucy."

Marcia didn't want her sister knowing that she and Quentin had been together for the last three days. "Hello, Lucy," she said coolly.

"I won't keep you. I just wanted to check up that you were doing all right out there—I hadn't realized Quentin had come back early. That's neat. He's a pretty special guy, isn't he?"

"No, it hasn't rained here at all," Marcia said smoothly. "What's the weather been like in the city?"

"I can take a hint," Lucy grumbled. "But he was the best friend to me that anyone could have been that summer on Shag Island, and don't you forget it. By the way, Cat left a message on my machine asking for your number out there, so I left it on her machine. How did we ever organize our lives before answering machines? So she'll probably be calling you too. When are you coming back to Ottawa?"

"I don't know yet."

"Stay all weekend. Troy and I can always go to the movies by ourselves on Saturday night. Glad you're having a good time, Marcie. Bye."

Marcia put down the receiver. Lucy, if she had her way, would have Marcia and Quentin married off in no time. As she was standing there frowning down at the telephone it rang again. With a strange sense of fatalism, she picked up the receiver. "Hello?"

"Cat here, Marcia. I'm in a bind and Lucy told me on Monday you had a week off. Could you come into town and stay at my place to look after Lydia's dogs until Sunday night?"

Catherine rarely wasted time on pleasantries but she rarely asked for favors either. "What's going on?" Marcia temporized.

"I've been given a flight to New York and back with a hotel reservation and three theater tickets included— my friend Lois was supposed to go and she's just had her appendix out. Too bad for her, but great for me. But I can only go if someone'll look after the dogs."

"When would I have to come?"

"Tonight."

She'd have to leave here right away. Leave Quentin. Which would be a very sensible thing to do. She was getting in deeper by the minute where that man was concerned, and a little breathing space wouldn't hurt at all. Trying to ignore all the contradictory emotions that the prospect of leaving Quentin caused her, Marcia said, "Sure, I'll do that."

"You're an angel," Cat said fervently. "Mother has my spare key—you could get it from her. I'll leave a note about the dogs. The big one's called Tansy, and I swear she was born without most of her brain cells—too highly bred, if you ask me. But Artie's really sweet. Thanks, Marcia. I'll be back Sunday around four."

"Have a good time," Marcia said, but she spoke into a hum on the wire; Cat had already cut the connection.

She replaced the receiver in its cradle and turned to face Quentin. His eyes were watchful. "What's up?" he said.

"Cat wants me to stay at her place until Sunday, to look after a friend's dogs. I'll have to leave right away."

From Marcia's brief contribution to the conversation, he had guessed something of the kind. Tamping down anger, he said, "You can hire people to do stuff like that."

"It's a last-minute thing. And anyway, Cat hardly ever asks me to do anything for her—she invented the word independent."

"I don't want you to go."

Marcia said carefully, "I think it's a good idea if I go, Quentin. We both need to cool—"

"Speak for yourself."

"All right, then," she said in a clipped voice, "I need time away from you. You're too intense. Too much has happened too fast. I need to get away and think about it all."

"You've been thinking instead of feeling all your life. The last thing you need to do right now is think."

"So I can't tell you what to do, but you can tell me? Thanks a lot."

She looked as though she'd like to throw the phone at him. Quentin swallowed hard and said in a more conciliatory tone, "Look, I'm doing a lousy job here. Can we start again? Why don't I come with you to Catherine's? I could help you with the dogs."

It was one thing to share a house with him in the country, another thing in the city with her family all around. "No thanks," she said. "I really need some time by myself."

"That's the old Marcia speaking. Not the real woman."

"Quit diagnosing me!"

"You're running away from everything that's happened since you came here. Keeping busy so you won't have to come face to face with yourself. Let alone with me."

"We're opposites!" she cried. "I'm tidy; you're messy. I'm a scientist; you're an artist. I'm from the city and you're from the country. I like pasta and you like steak. Don't you see? We're too different."

"How about this version?" he rapped. "You support a hospital and I support an orphanage. I love my job and you love yours. I want to go to bed with you and you want to go to bed with me. We're not so very different, not in the ways that count."

"I don't want to go—"

"You didn't like it when Paul and Lester lied to you. So don't lie to me."

He had an answer for everything. Angrier than she'd ever been in her life, Marcia said tightly, "As soon as I get packed I'm going into town. I really wish we didn't fight so much."

"You live alone and so do I, and we're both used to making our own decisions. That's one reason we're fighting and it's one more thing we have in common," he said with a wolfish grin.

"One more reason we should stop seeing each other." She hadn't known she was going to say that; her stomach clenched as if cold fingers had wrapped themselves around it.

"Let me tell you something else! You can hide my paintings if you like—I noticed one was missing from the bedroom. It had too much emotion in it, didn't it? It was too real. But don't think you can dispose of me so easily. Because I'm not just fighting for me, I'm fighting for you as well.'

"Nobody asked you to do that!"

"I'm beginning to think that Paul and Lester deserve my sympathy," Quentin grated. "You do what you like. I'm going out back to stack some wood."

The only good thing about all this, thought Marcia with icy clarity, was that she was much too angry even to think of crying. She stomped upstairs and packed in record time, hung the abstract back on the bedroom wall and poked her tongue out at it—an immature gesture that gave her considerable satisfaction—then shoved her books into her plastic cooler. He could keep the food. It would make a change from steak.

She lugged everything outside and loaded the trunk and the back seat of her car. From behind the house she could hear the steady thunk of log against log. She should say goodbye. She didn't want to say goodbye. She got in her car and turned the key.

CHAPTER SEVEN

THE ignition gave a faint click, but nothing happened. Marcia tried again. The motor didn't even turn over. Tight-jawed, she sat still for a minute or two, with some vague notion that she might have flooded the engine. Although how could she have if the motor hadn't turned over? She pushed the accelerator to the floor a couple of times, put the clutch in neutral and turned the key again. Still nothing.

"You would have to let me down now, wouldn't you?" she seethed, glaring at the gas gauge as though it were a face. "You couldn't have waited until I was in the city, with a nice garage down the street. Oh, no. *Now* what am I going to do?"

"Trouble, Marcia?" Quentin asked blandly.

She didn't even look up. "My car won't go," she said with noticeable restraint.

"Maybe if you got out and kicked it?"

"It'd probably fall apart if I did that. Although it would make *me* feel a whole lot better."

"Looks as though I'll have to drive you into town," he said.

She made the mistake of looking up. Wood chips were clinging to his T-shirt, which was clinging to his chest. His hands and his jeans were dirty and his eyes were laughing at her. Determined not to let the corners of her mouth curve upwards in response, she said crossly, "You've got bits of wood in your hair."

"I need a good woman to look after me."

"Someone to darn your socks and iron your shirts? You're in the wrong century."

"Someone to warm my bed on cold winter nights," he said. "Is your trunk locked? I'll transfer your stuff to my car."

What choice did she have?

Marcia got out of her car, rolled up the window and reached in the back seat for the cooler. Ten minutes later, with Quentin now in clean jeans and an open-necked shirt, they turned onto the highway. They traveled in silence for a few miles, then Marcia said stiffly, "Thank you for driving me in. I appreciate it."

"So you should—considering it's against my own best interests."

Marcia had had time to cool down. Very briefly she rested her hand on Quentin's knee. "I'm sorry I was so bitchy. It's not like me to keep losing my temper all the time. But seriously, Quentin—everything's happening too fast. I do need some time to myself."

"Can I phone you on the weekend?"

"I—I guess so."

With suppressed violence he said, "Just don't shut me out—that scares the hell out of me."

"I just wish you weren't so intense!"

"I'm the way I am," he retorted. "All your detachment and control, it's not working for you anymore. I'd bet my last dollar it's your own intensity you're so afraid of—and if I'm wrong, you can laugh all the way back to your city condo."

Marcia had no answer for him. She locked her fingers together in her lap and stared out the window; she didn't speak again until she had to give him directions to her mother's house. He pulled up behind a sleek black Mercedes and said briefly, "I'll wait out here."

She'd been afraid he'd want to go in with her. She ran up the walk and rang the doorbell. When no one came, impatiently she pressed it again. She was about to ring for the third time when Evelyn Barnes opened the door just a fraction.

"Marcia!" she exclaimed. "What—? Oh, my goodness, the key. I'd forgotten all about it." She shot a hunted glance over her shoulder. "What on earth did I—? You'd better come in."

She was wearing a long silk robe, exquisitely embroidered, her cheeks were flushed and her invitation had lacked any real welcome. "Sorry, Mother," Marcia said. "Perhaps I should have phoned. Are you getting ready to go out?"

Evelyn blushed, her cheeks a deep, rosy pink. "No— no, I'm not. Not really," she said incoherently, her eyes looking anywhere but at her daughter.

"Is there anything wrong?" Marcia said sharply, reaching out a hand to touch her mother's wrist.

Evelyn stepped back. "No! I'm just... Now where did I put that key? It's around here somewhere."

Evelyn was usually the most self-possessed of women. Puzzled and obscurely hurt, Marcia stayed in the hall. From where she was standing she could see into the living room. With a tiny shock she saw a man's jacket thrown over one of the chairs and a glorious bunch of tulips on the coffee-table in her mother's favorite crystal vase. Henry, she thought blankly. Henry's here. That's why Mother's so upset. That black Mercedes must be his.

He's upstairs. Upstairs in my mother's bed.

That's why it took her so long to answer the door. And why she's wearing a robe.

Her one desire to leave, Marcia tried to still the tangle of emotions in her breast and waited in an agony of impatience. Finally Evelyn hurried back into the hall. "I'd left it in the kitchen," she said, dropping the key into her daughter's palm. "Sorry I kept you waiting—I expect you're in a hurry to get to Cat's."

It was less than a subtle hint from a woman known for her hospitality. But Marcia had no wish to linger. She muttered, "Thanks . . . take care," and ran down the steps.

But Quentin was—of course—still waiting for her. Quentin, with his artist's eye that didn't miss a trick. She schooled her face to the detachment he was always accusing her of, and more sedately walked toward him. Climbing into the car, she said, "Keep going down this street to the second set of lights, then turn left," and took her time adjusting her seat belt.

"Anything the matter? You didn't stay long."

"She was getting ready to go out," Marcia said, despairing herself for the lie but knowing that she couldn't possibly tell him the truth. My mother was in bed with her lover. How would that sound? The fact that it was broad daylight made it all the worse.

What a prude she was.

If Quentin knew the truth, he'd tell her that it was her own sexuality she was afraid of, not her mother's. He'd be wrong, Marcia thought vehemently, absolutely wrong. But oh, God, how she longed to be by herself. She'd never realized how exhausting emotion could be. Terror, passion, happiness, rage, jealousy, shock . . . she'd experienced them all in the space of a few short days and she needed a break. She'd rent a mindless video tonight and she'd forget the whole lot of them: her mother, Henry, Lucy and Quentin. Most of all Quentin.

"Left again at the intersection," she said hastily.

Cat's house was on a quiet, tree-lined street, and was in immaculate condition. As Marcia walked up the front path she could already hear barking from inside: a bass and a soprano, she though drily, wondering if the neighbors had complained about the noise yet. She unlocked the door and pushed her suitcase in ahead of her. A big brown and white dog, its eyes peering through a thick fringe, ran at her joyously and planted its front feet on her chest, its pink tongue aimed for her nose. She ducked and said authoritatively, "Down!"

The dog licked her chin and shifted its paws to her shoulders. "You," said Marcia, "must be Tansy." She dropped her suitcase and put the paws back on the floor. Tansy grabbed at the handle of her suitcase and tried to drag it into the kitchen, growling ferociously.

"Are you sure you don't want me to stay?" Quentin drawled.

She looked around. He was carrying the cooler and her jacket; he looked large and solid and capable. I'm going to miss you, she thought unhappily. "I have a better idea," she said. "You can take Tansy back to the cottage with—"

The suitcase collided with a small table in the hall. As the table tottered Marcia grabbed for the pottery vase that was sitting on top of it. The table crashed to the floor, Tansy gave a yelp of terror and scrambled under the kitchen table, and Artie, a rather elderly Scottie, growled his displeasure. His was the bass voice. Marcia put the vase down on the floor and said, "My sentiments exactly, Artie."

Artie wagged his stub of a tail and waddled up to sniff her outstretched hand. Quentin put her belongings down on the pale blue carpet and made his way into the kitchen. Tansy made a rush for his ankles. "Stay," Quentin ordered. To Marcia's extreme annoyance Tansy stopped dead in her tracks and gazed adoringly into Quentin's eyes.

"You do have a way with females," Marcia remarked.

"So why doesn't it work with you?" He fished a scrap of paper out of his pocket and read out Cat's number from the telephone on the wall, copying it on the paper. Nothing underhanded about Quentin, Marcia thought shrewishly. I wonder how soon after he leaves here he'll start phoning.

The hall clock chimed the hour. Faintly surprised that it was so late, Marcia sat down hard on the nearest kitchen chair. "I should invite you for supper," she said. "Especially since you drove me all the way into town. I know I should."

"But you're not going to." To his own surprise as much as Marcia's, Quentin suddenly banged his fist on the table. Artie gave a startled yelp and Tansy made another theatrical dive for the table. Quentin said furiously, "I'm pushing you too hard, I know I am—I can't seem to help myself. But when I leave you like this I'm scared I'll never see you again, and that's the plain and unadorned truth. Have dinner with me on Saturday."

She gripped the edges of the chair and said steadily, "Quentin, I don't want to see you on the weekend. I need time out. A rest. An intermission. A break. Call it what you like."

"On Monday you go back to work. And we both know what that means."

The lab seemed like another world, remote and insignificant. "Then maybe next weekend," Marcia said.

"Maybe—is that the best you can do?"

Her own temper rose to meet his. "Yes."

"Fine. If I'm still around, I'll give you a call. If not, I'll send you a postcard. From Peru. Or Australia. Or the North Pole." He hauled her to her feet, planted a kiss of mingled rage and desire somewhere in the vicinity of her mouth, and marched out of the room. The front door slammed. Marcia sat down again and Tansy raised her aristocratic nose to the ceiling and let out a howl worthy of a coyote.

"I'm not going to cry," said Marcia. "I absolutely refuse to."

Nor, by a superhuman effort, did she.

He wouldn't go to Peru...would he?

That evening Marcia drank cup after cup of herbal tea and indulged in some long-overdue reflection. By nine o'clock she'd worked out that her mother had been afraid to tell her eldest daughter the truth about Henry. She's scared of me, thought Marcia in dismay. Scared to be real with me. Because I've been sending out messages for years not to bother me, please, that I'm busy with more important matters than family and intimacy... I haven't been a very good daughter.

Not giving herself time to think, because if she did she might rationalize her way out of it, she picked up the phone and dialed her mother's number. "Evelyn Barnes," her mother said briskly.

"Mother, it's Marcia." She licked her lips, horribly nervous, and said idiotically, "How are you?" Then in a rush she went on, "I didn't call you to ask that. I wanted to tell you that I figured out Henry was there and I—"

"I should have told you. But somehow I couldn't."

"Mother, it's fine with me—truly it is. I want you to be happy. That's all."

There was a long silence during which Marcia listened to the racing of her heart and felt her palm clutch the receiver. Yet she knew she had spoken the simple truth. Evelyn said slowly, "Why, Marcia...that's very sweet of you."

"Henry seems like a really nice man; I'm so glad for you. I'm only sorry I've kept you at such a distance all these years that you didn't feel comfortable telling me about it."

Evelyn gave a sudden throaty chuckle. "Well, you know, it's very new to me too. At my age, to fall in love! Some days I feel like a sixteen-year-old, Marcia. It's so wonderful." She hesitated. "So if we were to announce our engagement, you wouldn't mind?"

"Mind?" Marcia said warmly. "I'd be delighted. We'll throw a big party to welcome Henry into the family."

"Oh, Marcie, I'm so glad you phoned," Evelyn gulped. "Here I am weeping and it's only because I'm happy. I was afraid you wouldn't approve, I guess. That you'd think I was too old... We thought we'd get married before Lucy and Troy go back to Vancouver—do you think that's a good idea? Originally I was planning a very quiet ceremony with just a couple of witnesses, but Henry says he's so proud of me he wants all our friends and relatives to take part."

"Henry's absolutely right," Marcia announced. "I'll help you with the planning—I'd love to do that." She would, she thought in amazement. It would be fun.

"We'll let you know the date as soon as we've settled on it. Marcie dear, thanks so much."

Marcia cleared her throat. "A big hello to Henry. And my love to you, Mother."

"Thanks, darling. I love you too. Bye for now."

I'm crying again, thought Marcia, and blew her nose. Making changes is hard work. But worth it. Definitely worth it.

On Friday, in between more bouts of concentrated thinking, Marcia walked the dogs—a perilous proceeding as Tansy had no road sense and was possessed by the need to greet personally every man, woman, child, cat and dog that she came across. She was also, Marcia discovered, disconcertingly strong.

Marcia tried taking the dogs four times that day, hoping to wear Tansy out. But Tansy's energy bordered on the manic, and Artie with his short legs and Marcia with her longer ones were the ones who ended up worn out.

PLAY
HARLEQUIN'S
LUCKY HEARTS GAME

GAME

AND YOU GET

★ **FREE BOOKS**

★ **A FREE GIFT**

★ **AND MUCH MORE**

TURN THE PAGE AND
DEAL YOURSELF IN

PLAY "LUCKY HEARTS" AND YOU GET...

★ Exciting Harlequin Presents® novels—FREE

★ PLUS a Lovely Simulated Pearl Drop Necklace—FREE

THEN CONTINUE YOUR LUCKY STREAK WITH A SWEETHEART OF A DEAL

1. Play Lucky Hearts as instructed on the opposite page.

2. Send back this card and you'll receive brand-new Harlequin Presents® novels. These books have a cover price of $3.50 each, but they are yours to keep absolutely free.

3. There's no catch. You're under no obligation to buy anything. We charge nothing — ZERO — for your first shipment. And you don't have to make any minimum number of purchases — not even one!

4. The fact is thousands of readers enjoy receiving books by mail from the Harlequin Reader Service. They like the convenience of home delivery…they like getting the best new novels months BEFORE they're available in stores…and they love our discount prices!

5. We hope that after receiving your free books you'll want to remain a subscriber. But the choice is yours — to continue or cancel, anytime at all! So why not take us up on our invitation, with no risk of any kind. You'll be glad you did!

*This lovely necklace will add glamour to your most elegant outfit! Its cobra-link chain is a generous 18" long, and its lustrous simulated cultured pearl is mounted in an attractive pendant! Best of all, it's **absolutely free**, just for accepting our no-risk offer.*

HARLEQUIN'S

With a coin— scratch off the silver card and check below to see what we have for you.

YES! I have scratched off the silver card. Please send me all the free books and gift for which I qualify. I understand that I am under no obligation to purchase any books, as explained on the back and on the opposite page.

106 CIH A6PC (U-H-P-01/97)

NAME

ADDRESS   APT.

CITY   STATE   ZIP

Twenty-one gets you 4 free books, and a free simulated pearl drop necklace

Twenty gets you 4 free books

Nineteen gets you 3 free books

Eighteen gets you 2 free books

Offer limited to one per household and not valid to current Harlequin Presents® subscribers. All orders subject to approval.

© 1991 HARLEQUIN ENTERPRISES LIMITED.   **PRINTED IN U.S.A.**

THE HARLEQUIN READER SERVICE®: HERE'S HOW IT WORKS

Accepting free books places you under no obligation to buy anything. You may keep the books and gift and return the shipping statement marked "cancel". If you do not cancel, about a month later we'll send you 6 additional novels, and bill you just $2.90 each plus 25¢ delivery per book and applicable sales tax, if any.* That's the complete price–and compared to cover prices of $3.50 each–quite a bargain! You may cancel at any time, but if you choose to continue, every month we'll send you 6 more books, which you may either purchase at the discount price…or return to us and cancel your subscription.

*Terms and prices subject to change without notice. Sales tax applicable in N.Y.

If offer card is missing, write to: Harlequin Reader Service, 3010 Walden Ave., P.O. Box 1867, Buffalo, NY 14240-1867

In the morning she arranged to have her car towed to the garage. In the evening she went shopping. Her wardrobe, she decided, reflected her personality. Safe, conservative and dull. In the Sparks Street Mall she found a swirling gored skirt and a cowl-necked top in a gorgeous shade of raspberry-red, and in a trendy boutique she bought a white silk shirt and a pair of very flattering designer jeans, along with a Mexican silver belt and some turquoise jewelry.

She then decided that if she was going to look different outwardly she should also be more adventurous from the skin out, and spent three-quarters of an hour and rather a lot of money in a lingerie shop. She'd had no idea bras and panties were so pretty—flowered, lacy, all the colors of the rainbow. It was a long time since she'd browsed like this, she concluded. Too long.

Loaded up with her packages, she went home and phoned Lucy to tell her that she was free to babysit for them Saturday evening. "Come for supper," Lucy said. "On Saturdays we usually order out—no fuss, no muss. How's Quentin?"

"Fine, I guess."

"You guess," Lucy snorted. "If I'd known Cat wanted you back in town, I wouldn't have given her your number. Tell you what, why don't I see if Mother and Henry will babysit? Then you and Quentin could come to the movie with us."

"No," said Marcia.

"Marcie, one of these days you're going to wake up and find out that life has passed you by," Lucy flared. "Regret makes a cold bedfellow. I discovered that when Troy and I were separated. I'll see you tomorrow. Bye." She banged the receiver down in Marcia's ear.

Quentin had slammed the door and now Lucy was slamming down the telephone. It would be nice, Marcia thought, if other people weren't quite so sure that they knew what was good for her.

But if Lucy had suggested inviting Quentin to the movies, then presumably he hadn't gone to Peru.

Not yet, anyway.

She brewed another pot of herbal tea and sat in the tiny patch of sunlight on Cat's deck. Artie flopped at her feet and Tansy tore round the yard looking for a gap in the fence, barked at the maple tree and tried to climb in Marcia's lap. Finally she, too, subsided on the plank floor.

Shutting her mind to the conversation with Lucy, Marcia thought about Jason and Jason's mother, and about the muskrat, and about how long it had been since she'd walked through a field of wildflowers, or even sat on a deck in the sun. She thought about the hospital in India, so very worthwhile and so very far away. Too far for emotional involvement. She thought about her mother and Henry, who would be her stepfather in just a couple of months. The only person she didn't think about was Quentin.

She didn't want to think about Quentin.

That night she dreamed again. The same nightmare where she was drowning in the swirling currents of a deep blue sea. She sat up in bed, trying to quell the racing of her heart. I'm in terror of Quentin and of all he represents, she thought with the clarity of extreme fear. That's why I don't want to think about him. If I let him into my life, really let him in, I'm afraid I'll disappear, that I'll lose myself.

According to Quentin—and to Lucy—she'd find herself. Could that be true? And what if she made love with him ... what then? She'd never be able to go back to the way she was.

What if he were here now, beside her in the bed, in the opaque darkness of a city night? What would happen?

Her body sprang to life and her imagination began to gallop down pathways scarcely known to her. In utter exasperation Marcia went downstairs, made herself a peanut butter sandwich and watched a very silly movie on TV; at seven in the morning she woke up on the chesterfield with a crick in her neck and the television still bleating.

She snapped it off. Men, she thought vengefully. Or rather, one particular man. A man who built wonderful houses that let the sunshine in, who painted people's emotions, who kissed her as if there was no tomorrow. Quentin knew what he wanted.

He wanted her, Marcia. He'd made no secret of that.

Although he hadn't phoned her once since she'd come to Cat's.

Tansy whined horribly at the basement door and Artie gave the muted woof that meant he needed to go out. Cautiously Marcia moved her head from side to side, stretching her neck muscles. She was going to buy herself a new car that very morning. Which was undoubtedly a classic case of avoidance. Her mouth set, she headed for the basement door, bracing herself for Tansy's hysterical onslaught.

Her little gray car looked very dilapidated parked next to all the gleaming new models at the dealer's. But Marcia was feeling militant, and when she and the salesman parted company at noon, she felt she'd gotten a bargain. She drove out of the lot the proud owner of a bright red car no bigger than her old one but decidedly more noticeable. After she'd parked it in Cat's driveway and walked around it a couple of times, patting its sleek sides and admiring her reflection in the shiny chrome, she took the dogs for another walk.

Later that afternoon she drove her car to the apartment Troy and Lucy were renting for the summer; the paint on the car clashed with her raspberry-red outfit, which she'd decided to wear even though it was quite unsuitable for babysitting. It symbolized something. Something she wasn't yet ready to put into words.

"Wow!" said Lucy as she let her sister in the door. "Jazzy outfit. You're the best-dressed sitter in Ottawa... We've just ordered pizza—I hope you're hungry."

By the time they'd eaten pizza with the works, Lucy had also fed Chris his supper. In between mouthfuls he kept pushing his fingers into his mouth, whimpering. "He's teething again," Lucy said unhappily as Troy lifted him out of his high chair. "Troy, are you sure we should go? I hate leaving him like this."

Chris was snuffling into his father's shoulder. Marcia said, "Of course you should. I'm a doctor, after all."

"I forget that sometimes," Lucy said tactlessly. "Your job is so isolated from teething babies and over-protective mothers."

From reality, was what Lucy meant. Wincing inwardly, Marcia said, "Write down the phone number of the theater you're going to. If he's really upset I'll get in touch with you."

Lucy was chewing her lip; she looked tense and unsettled in a way Marcia was to remember. Troy said firmly, "Get your jacket, Lucy, or we'll be late." He then passed Chris to Marcia. "There's some stuff in the bathroom to rub on his gums. Thanks, sis."

Three minutes later the door closed behind them. Chris began to cry with a dedication that reminded Marcia of Tansy. She turned the radio to an easy listening station, then went to the bathroom, where she very gently rubbed his gums. He jammed his fist into his mouth. Crooning to him softly, she started making slow circles around the room in time with the music.

Half an hour later his forehead had drooped to her shoulder. He was heavy and her arms were aching. She was walking down the hall to put him in his crib when someone knocked sharply on the door. Marcia jumped. Chris's eyes jerked open and he let out a loud wail. Muttering a rude word under her breath, she went to see who it was.

Through the security peephole she saw Quentin standing on the other side of the door.

CHAPTER EIGHT

MARCIA'S heart gave a lunge in her chest. Clutching Chris to her breast like a shield, she unlocked the door and pulled it open. Quentin's face went blank with shock. Then joy blazed in his blue eyes and a grin split his face. "Marcia—so she invited you too! That's wonderful."

He was carrying a bottle of wine in the crook of his arm and he looked very handsome in a brown leather bomber jacket and faded jeans. Marcia stood back to let him in, watching as the joy in his face was replaced by puzzlement and then calculation. "You didn't know I was coming, did you? Where's Lucy?"

"Lucy and Troy have gone to a movie. I'm baby-sitting. I'll murder my darling sister when she gets home... Hush, sweetheart, it's all right."

Quentin closed the door behind him. "No dinner for three at seven-thirty?"

"No dinner at all. We ordered pizza and finished it off."

"Oh, well," he said cheerfully, "at least I've got a bottle of wine. Very good wine, if I do say so. I shall ply you with it."

"Babysitters aren't allowed to get sloshed, Quentin."

He quirked his brow. "You look utterly enchanting, dearest Marcia. I love the color of raspberries and your cheeks match your dress. What's wrong with Chris?"

"He's teething. He was nine-tenths asleep when you knocked on the door."

"He's not ten-tenths awake." Quentin shucked off his jacket; he was wearing a blue denim shirt under it, his

102

body hair a dark tangle in the V at his throat. "Here, give him to me for a while—he's been slobbering all over your dress. Is it a new dress?"

"I spent a whole lot of money between yesterday and today," Marcia said with a touch of defiance.

He shot her a quick glance as he settled the little boy into his shoulder. Then he said, "He's wet. Soaked. Come on, Dr. Barnes, that's your department."

"I never noticed," she said, flustered. "We can change him in the bedroom."

Chris's room was lit by a soft nightlight. As Marcia washed and changed him his wails turned to a full-bellied crying and his little face screwed up in misery. Quentin watched as Marcia fumbled with the lid of the petroleum jelly jar, dropped the baby powder and struggled with the tabs on the diapers. "Bet you haven't done that since medical school," he said.

"Pour me a glass of wine, Quentin," she retorted. "I can see it's going to be a long evening."

When she went back into the living room Quentin had lowered the lights, and two glasses of wine along with a hefty tuna sandwich were sitting on the coffee-table. A tunafish sandwich didn't go with seduction any more than a screaming baby did, thought Marcia. Not that Quentin was making any attempt to seduce her. "I'll hold him while you eat," she said.

Chris found his thumb and his screams subsided. She waltzed him round the room until her arms got tired. Then she sat down on the chesterfield a careful distance from Quentin. When he'd finished the sandwich he took the baby from her, easing him against his chest. "I won't bite, Marcia. Drink your wine and tell me about all this money you spent."

The wine was a full-bodied burgundy. Marcia let it slide down her throat and said, "I bought two outfits and a car, none of which is navy, brown or gray."

He gave a snort of laughter. "You don't do things by half measures, do you?"

Underneath her dress she was wearing raspberry-red lingerie. "No," she said demurely, "I don't."

"I find that encouraging... Hush, Chris, it's okay." Chris whimpered and attacked his thumb again; Quentin shifted himself more comfortably into the corner of the chesterfield and smiled at her. "You're sitting so far away I practically have to yell at you. Move over."

She gazed at him warily and took another gulp of wine, with scant respect for its quality. She looked very beautiful in her brave red dress, he thought; it made her skin creamy and darkened her eyes to purple. He said lightly, "I lust after you like a sailor who's been at sea for six months. Or an artist who hasn't been near a woman for a lot longer than that. But a ten-month-old baby who's teething is a most effective chaperon—I bet Lucy never thought of that when she set us up. So you're quite safe. I won't be seducing you on the chesterfield, the carpet or the coffee-table. More's the pity."

Marcia glowered at him. "I don't feel the slightest bit safe when you're anywhere in my vicinity."

"Tell me more. I like it."

She said in a rush, "I'm very glad you didn't go to Peru."

"So, right now, am I."

She was feeling rather peculiar; the spicy pizza was cohabiting with the red glow of the wine along with a strange ache somewhere deep inside her, which had nothing to do with food or drink and everything to do with the sight of Quentin holding her nephew. His big hand was curved protectively around Chris's body; Chris had butted his head under Quentin's chin, with his cheek lying on Quentin's chest. It was all too easy to imagine that she and Quentin were an ordinary married couple spending a quiet Saturday evening at home with their child; the ache increased in intensity.

"My mother's getting married again," she blurted. "To Henry."

"What brought that to mind?" he said softly.

"You have a positive genius for asking unanswerable questions! Did you like Henry?"

"I liked him very much. My left arm needs a counterbalance for my right. Come over here."

Marcia let another mouthful of wine course its way down her throat. Then she put her glass down and edged nearer, her back ramrod-straight. "It's not very romantic to entice a woman into your arms by calling her a counterbalance."

"Arm. Singular," Quentin said, and put it round her, his palm cupping her shoulder, his fingers beginning to caress it in a gentle, hypnotic rhythm. "Relax. I want to tell you a story."

Go for broke, thought Marcia, and drew her feet up on the chesterfield and let her head fall to his shoulder. His arm tightened instinctively. She closed her eyes, aware through every pore of the tautness of his muscles, the unyielding hardness of bone, the clean, masculine scent of his skin. "Not sure I'll be able to concentrate," she mumbled.

"Marcia..."

There was a quality in his voice that made her look up. His eyes were an unfathomable blue, and for a moment she felt a catch of fear. But when he found her mouth with his, fear dropped away as if it had never been. Wonderment and a bittersweet longing surged through her veins; she opened to the probing of his tongue and to a heat like that of a summer day.

He was drowning, Quentin thought, and wished Christopher Stephen Donovan a thousand miles away. Or at least asleep in his crib down the hall. She smelled so sweet, the silky brush of her hair against his cheek tantalizing all his senses. He felt her fingers creep up to stroke his nape, then bury themselves in his hair, and as his head began to reel he hoped fleetingly that Lucy was thoroughly enjoying the movie, because she'd sure done him a good turn.

Chris gave a little whimper, then sucked juicily on his thumb again. Nibbling at Quentin's lips in between her words, Marcia whispered, "I don't think babysitters are supposed to neck on the couch either... You were going to tell me a story."

"So I was."

As he lifted his hand to push her hair back from her face she saw that his fingers were unsteady. I do that to him, she thought humbly. I have that power. "Why me?" she burst out. "That's what I don't understand."

Was this really the right time to explain to her why he couldn't stay away from her? Or would it only frighten her away again? "That's what the story's about," he said. He leaned his head back on the chesterfield and closed his eyes, holding her close to his body. Where she belonged. He had to believe that.

"Once upon a time in the village of Holton there lived a boy called Quentin," he began. "He never had any brothers or sisters, but that didn't really bother him because he had the woods and the fields as his playground, and he'd spend hours watching deer and porcupines and birds—watching them and drawing them, because he always knew he was going to be an artist. And perhaps that was another reason he never missed having a sister or a brother. His other reason was because of his parents. They were as solid and dependable as granite, and as loving as the wild geese who mate for life and share the sky."

She felt a sudden stabbing pain—for had she not lost her father when she was five? "Yes?" she prompted.

Without noticing, Quentin changed pronouns. "I always knew there was something special about my parents—those two ordinary people who loved each other so passionately. The older I get, the rarer I think it is that a couple can sustain that kind of love through good times and bad... Lucy and Troy have managed to do it, although not without enormous difficulty. I expect that's partly why I'm friends with them."

He looked down at the woman curled so intimately into his body. "Ever since I was ten or eleven I've been sure I'd meet the right woman—the one who'd be my mate in the way my mother was my father's. My mistake was to ignore that certainty when I married Helen. But when you walked in the door of the gallery I knew you were the one. The woman I'd been waiting for most of my life." He cleared his throat. "End of story. Or should I say beginning?"

Marcia sat up straight. "You're in love with me? Is that what you're saying?"

"I suppose so. Although the words have become so damned trite I almost hate to say them. There's a connection between us, Marcia. Your blood calls to mine and mine to yours. Hell, I don't know how to say it— I deal in paint, not words." He thought for a moment. "Your image is my heart's image...maybe that's what I'm getting at."

Shaken, she said, "You really mean it, don't you?"

"Oh, yes." He traced the elegant arch of bone in her cheek with one finger; her eyes were as wary as those of a deer that smells danger. "I fought it for a while. Didn't think you were my type—control and detachment have never been high on my list, and Lucy had painted a picture of you back on the island that wasn't overly flattering." He paused. "It might have been an accurate picture then...but I don't think it is now."

Suddenly he'd had enough of words. Very deliberately his hand followed the slim line of her neck to her collarbone and the sweet rise of her breast, then fell to the flatness of her belly; when he reached the angle of her thigh he let it rest there, heavy and possessive on the soft raspberry-red fabric.

He heard her breath catch in her throat and watched her eyes dilate, and all the while she said not a word. "Red's the color of passion," he said softly. "Did you know that, Marcia?"

"We've neither of us made love with anyone for a long time, that's all this is!"

"You know better than that."

She did. "Are you saying I'm the woman you want to spend the rest of your life with?"

"Yeah," he said. "Yeah, that's what I'm saying."

"But we only met two weeks ago."

"Spend more time with me. That way we'll get to know each other."

She looked down at his hand where it rested on her leg; she already knew both its strength and its sensitivity. She reached over, picked up her glass of wine and drained it. "Why didn't you tell me this before?"

He felt his nerves tighten. "You weren't exactly receptive."

"You lied to me," she said sharply.

"I didn't! I just didn't tell you the whole truth."

"Now you're playing with words."

"Stop trying to pick a fight with me!" he roared. "You've got to be the most infuriating and obstinate woman that I know, and don't ask me why I'm in love with you because I don't have a clue—but just don't accuse me of lying to you because I won't stand for that."

Chris reared his head up. His jaw was agape and his gray eyes full of astonishment. "Hi there, buddy," said

Quentin in a more moderate voice. "You're cramping my style, you know that?"

Chris gave him a gleeful smile and blew a large, fat bubble. Marcia said helplessly, "I did it again. Lost my cool, I mean."

"Sexual deprivation—that's what it is."

She suddenly began to laugh, a delightful cascade of sound that made Quentin smile in spite of himself. "Take note," she chortled, "I'm actually agreeing with you, Quentin Ramsey. I'm announcing to the world that one of the effects you have on me—only one, mind you—is indeed that of sexual frustration."

With genuine interest Quentin asked, "What are the rest?"

She ticked off her fingers one by one. "Rage. Panic. Desire. Happiness. Misery. Jealousy. How am I doing?"

"You've left out detachment."

"Dear me, so I have."

Chris reached out for her, his smile revealing three pearl-like teeth and his red gums. Marcia took him in her arms, cuddling him and blowing down the neck of his pajamas. He gave his fat laugh and blew another bubble.

Quentin said in a peculiar voice, "When I see you like that it's all too easy to imagine Chris is ours. Can you picture yourself as the mother of my child, Marcia?"

With an honesty that entranced him, she announced, "Most of the time I'm with you I seem to be pre-occupied to the exclusion of all else with the process that makes babies. But when I see you holding Chris I get this funny ache inside." She grimaced. "This has got to be the wackiest conversation I've ever had in my whole life. I've never even lived with a man, Quentin. The day-to-day stuff. Who does the dishes? Who cleans the bathroom sink? I bet we'd drive each other crazy inside of a month."

"One way to find out. Move out to the cottage," he said promptly.

"You don't mean that!"

The mere thought of living with her made his throat tight and his mouth dry. "I sure do."

She gaped at him much as Chris had. "Do you know what's really wacky here? That I'm actually considering it."

"All you've got to say is yes. Not a complicated word."

His crooked smile did funny things to Marcia's heart-rate, which was already erratic enough. As Chris seized a handful of her hair she said unevenly, "I think we should give him a bottle and put him to bed. Lucy won't thank us if we keep him up half the night."

"Don't change the subject. Say yes."

"Will you hold him while I warm his bottle?" Staring into Chris's slate-gray irises, so like his father's, she added rapidly, "I promise I'll give you an answer by the end of next week. I promise. Don't rush me, Quentin...please."

The soft lamplight feel on the swell of her breast and the delicate hollow in her wrist; both filled Quentin with a longing that made nonsense of patience and promises. A longing he had to keep to himself so he wouldn't frighten her away. He was rushing her. He knew he was. But how could he help it? He got to his feet and tossed back the better part of a glass of wine. Then he took the baby from her, being careful not to touch her because she wasn't his—not yet. And maybe never.

Her hand fell on his arm. "When you look like that, I...I'm sorry, Quentin, I know it doesn't make any sense to you to wait for a week, but I have to be sure I'm doing the right thing. This is serious, what we're talking about, and it scares me out of my wits. Please try and understand."

He said roughly, "Do you know what I hate here? That I've got no choice. I'll wait because I have to wait. Because you're the woman I want and no other will do." He gave a harsh laugh. "When I was eleven it never occurred to me that love might feel like a trap. Closing in on me. Cutting off my options. How's that for male arrogance—not to realize that the woman I wanted might not want me?"

Frightened by the tone of their voices, Chris began to whimper again. Restlessly Quentin moved his shoulders, trying to work the tension out of them. "I think I'll go, Marcia. It's not fair to upset Chris, and we're getting nowhere fast."

"I don't want you to go!"

"So we're both caught," he said heavily.

"Maybe love's only sweetness and light when you're not in it," Marcia said, not very sensibly.

"You don't get much of anything without a cost—I know that. I've always been a nomad, wandering wherever the spirit took me. Loving you means losing that freedom—although I'm not so sure that I wouldn't discover another kind of freedom."

"I'd lose some of my independence," she said in a small voice. "Most of my life I've done what I want to do—no one else to consult, nobody else's schedule to consider. That would change, wouldn't it?" She gave him a sly grin. "Knowing you."

"We'd gain so much more than we'd lose," he said forcefully.

She began walking up and down, her skirt swirling round her legs, her stockinged feet whispering on the carpet. "Do you know when my safe little world started to collapse? When Lucy and Troy's first baby died— Michael. I'd envied them their happiness—they were so in love with each other and then they had Michael, this perfect little baby. But Michael died and the marriage

fell apart and they were both so unhappy—it was awful.
Even though I was just an onlooker, I think that's when
I finally started growing up."

Her hands were deep in the pockets of her skirt and
her shoulders were hunched. Quentin stood still, each
word she spoke making him more and more certain of
the depths of passion buried in her heart. The red dress
was no accident. He said quietly, "I love you, Marcia."

She stopped dead in her tracks. "It's too soon,
Quentin," she said desperately. "I'm doing the best I
can—but it's just too soon."

His impatience battled with his reason; the latter won
by a narrow margin. "Let's put Chris to bed and then
I'll get out of here. And maybe in the next couple of
days we can have a date. An ordinary date." He smiled.
"Pizza and a movie, for instance."

His reward was to see her smile back—a rather wan
smile, but a smile nevertheless. "Sounds good," she said.

Half an hour later Chris was settled in his crib and
Quentin had shrugged on his jacket. Marcia was standing
in the hall, the overhead light shining on her face in which
tension, uncertainty and a tremulous happiness all had
their place. "I feel—" she began, then she suddenly flung
herself at him, wrapping her arms tightly around his
waist and hugging him as hard as if he were leaving for
South America rather than the Gatineau Hills.

Quentin's heart was pounding in his chest like the
thunk of an ax on wood. He strained her to him, lifting
her off her feet and kissing her in fierce gratitude and
even fiercer love, and evidently he felt her respond to
him just as fiercely. He thrust with his tongue. As she
dug her nails into his scalp and pressed her body into
his he knew that he had already moved into that new
freedom of which he had spoken.

Behind them a key turned in the lock. Quentin raised
his head, watching the door open, and dropped Marcia

unceremoniously to the floor. But when Lucy's head came round the door his arms were still linked around Marcia's waist, and her hands were clutching the front of his shirt as though that was all that was keeping her upright.

With rather overdone surprise Lucy said, "Why, Quentin, how nice to see you."

Marcia stepped back, her cheeks redder than any raspberry. "He was just leaving," she said.

"The movie was awful," Lucy went on trenchantly. "Neither of us could stand it, so we left."

Troy looked from Marcia to Quentin in amusement. "Take off your jacket and stay awhile, Quentin. How's Chris?"

"He settled down a few minutes ago," Marcia babbled. "We gave him another bottle—I hope that was all right. He seemed to be hungry."

"Whatever works," said Troy, the specialist in pediatrics.

Much as he liked Lucy and Troy, Quentin wasn't in the mood for small talk about movies and teething babies, nor for dealing with Lucy's curiosity about what had been going on between him and her sister. He said, "I think I'll head back to the cottage. I'll give you a call tomorrow at Cat's, Marcia—take care." Without hurrying, he kissed her open mouth, smiled impartially at all three of them and let himself out.

He ran down the stairs, whistling loudly to himself. One reason he didn't want to deal with Lucy was because he wasn't as sure as he'd like to be of what was going on between him and Marcia. He loved her. No question of that. If only he were as sure that she loved him back.

Still, he felt immeasurably more confident of the outcome than he had twenty-four hours ago.

And that, for now, was enough.

CHAPTER NINE

ON SUNDAY morning Marcia took the dogs for a walk. When she got back, the light on Cat's answering machine was blinking. She pressed the button and Quentin's voice surged into the kitchen.

"Marcia," he said abruptly. "I hate these bloody machines. I'm always afraid they're going to cut me off before I've finished. I'm going out in the canoe for a while—my dreams were such that I require large expanses of cold water. I'll call you later. Maybe we could have dinner together tonight? I never know whether to say goodbye—I mean, who the dickens am I saying goodbye to? You're not even there. I love you."

The machine beeped. Marcia picked Artie up, hugged him and put him down again. "Am I in love with that man?" she said. "This is nothing like the way I felt about Lester. Or Paul."

Artie woofed. Tansy whined. And Marcia put on a CD of operatic arias and warbled along with them as she cleaned up Cat's house and packed her own clothes. She showered and put on her new jeans and silk shirt, along with the Mexican belt and a big pair of silver and turquoise earrings. She then applied more make-up than usual and brushed her hair smooth. Not bad, she thought complacently, looking at herself in the bathroom mirror.

Would Quentin like her new shirt? Surely there'd be no harm in having a meal with him tonight. And Lucy had suggested that all four of them go out for dinner on Tuesday; Evelyn had offered to stay with her grandson so that Henry could get to know him. Humming to herself, she made a salad and wished Quentin would phone. He'd been canoeing an awfully long time.

Was worrying about someone another side of love?

Was she in love with Quentin?

In love or not, one more thing the two of them had in common was impatience. She hated waiting, too.

Tansy was racing around Cat's small back garden, tearing up little chunks of sod with her claws, and Artie was sitting under the sundial, watching. She'd take them for one last walk to pass the time until Quentin phoned.

Not bothering to change, Marcia picked up the leashes and went outside. As usual, Tansy went nearly berserk at the prospect of an outing. After a brief tussle, which Marcia won, the three of them set off down the sidewalk.

The sun was shining and Marcia felt extraordinarily happy. She marched along, every now and then stopping to untangle Tansy's leash from whatever obstacle she'd wrapped herself around. Artie plodded phlegmatically at Marcia's side. She would miss Artie; she didn't think she'd miss Tansy.

Half an hour later Marcia turned around to go home. Thinking rather more about Quentin than about the dogs, she didn't see the lustrous-coated Great Dane standing on the opposite curb beside its elegant female owner, the pair of them waiting with equal poise for the light to change. But Tansy saw the Great Dane and her eyes lit up.

She made a sudden lunge for the street. Pulled off balance, Marcia was jerked out of her daydream. As she staggered sideways, grabbing for the lightpole, the leash was yanked from her hand. To her horror she saw Tansy leap into the road. "Tansy!" she yelled. "Tansy, come back!"

With a screech of brakes and a pungent smell of burnt rubber a black sedan came to a halt across the white line. But not soon enough. As though it were happening in a dream, Marcia saw Tansy's hairy brown and white body make a lazy curve in the air and thud to the tarmac. For a split second she was frozen to the spot. Then she looked from side to side and raced out into the street, dragging Artie with her.

Tansy's eyes were closed. She was bleeding from a cut in her side. Marcia gathered the dog into her arms and heard a male voice say, "I'm most terribly sorry, but I really couldn't stop in time."

The driver of the black sedan was standing beside her. He looked rather as she had first pictured Quentin, she thought dazedly, right down to the tweed jacket, the pipe and the British accent. A younger man on a bicycle had begun competently directing traffic. The man in the tweed jacket said, "Please allow me to drive you to the veterinarian's—there's a clinic only two blocks from here."

The black sedan was a Jaguar. "Thank you." Marcia stumbled over the words. "I'll try not to make a mess in your car."

"This way, madam."

Within ten minutes the veterinarian on call was opening the door of the clinic and the man in the tweed jacket had driven away. Clutching Artie to her, Marcia sat trembling on the bench. Twenty minutes later the vet, a very pretty young woman, came back into the waiting area. "The dog will be fine," she said. "Concussion, so I'll keep her until tomorrow for observation, and ten stitches in her side. But no broken bones or internal damage. She was very lucky."

Holding tight to her self-control, Marcia paid the bill, left Cat's name and phone number, and took a cab back to her sister's house.

A yellow sportscar she would have recognized anywhere was parked at the curb and Quentin was sitting on the front steps of Cat's house. He stood up as she got out of the cab and started down the path toward her. Then he halted, and said in a strangled voice, "Marcia, what's happened? There's blood all over your shirt."

"It's Tansy's; she ran out into the road," Marcia said, and felt her body begin to tremble again.

"Sweetheart," he said, a note in his voice she hadn't heard before. "Here, give me the key—and Artie."

He put an arm around her waist, unlocked the door, let Artie in and stood aside so Marcia could enter. Cat had a large antique mirror in the hall. Marcia quavered, "I bought this shirt the same day I bought the red dress. It's ruined."

"For God's sake, it's only a shirt! For a minute I thought it was your blood."

He did look pale, she noticed absently. Wringing her hands, she said, "How will I ever tell Cat? It was all my fault. I wasn't thinking about what I was doing and Tansy ran out into the street and got hit by a car."

"Was she badly hurt?"

"No—oh, no. She'll be fine. But I was responsible, don't you see?"

She looked utterly distraught. Quentin said carefully, "Tansy is an unmitigated idiot and you'd have to be Superwoman to keep her under control."

"I said I'd look after her. And I didn't."

He wasn't at all sure what she was getting at. He rested a hand on her shoulder, but she pulled away from him. "Marcia, what's going on here? Accidents happen and we all make mistakes—you're only human. How about putting some of the responsibility on Tansy's owner, who didn't train her, or on the kennels, who must have been inbreeding dogs for generations? Or even on Cat, who didn't really warn you what you were getting into."

Marcia was backed against the wall, shrinking from him as though he were an enemy. "I'm responsible," she repeated, and two tears dropped from her lashes to trickle down her cheeks.

Quentin couldn't stand to see her cry. He stepped closer, swung her into his arms and headed for the stairs. "What are you doing?" Marcia squeaked.

"I'm taking you upstairs. I'm going to start a bath for you, then I'll wash your shirt in the kitchen sink."

She was beating against his chest with her fists. "I don't want you taking over my life, do you hear me? Telling me what to do. Interfering all the time. Put me down this minute!"

"No," said Quentin. "Stop hitting me."

"Put me down and I will."

"For once you're going to do what I say and not what you want! A new experience, Marcia. It'll be good for you." Her fist hit his breastbone. "Ouch, that hurts."

"Good," she seethed as he pushed open the bathroom door with his foot and lowered her to the floor. "Go home, Quentin—I don't want you here."

He felt suddenly cold. "You don't mean that."

"I do! I've looked after myself for over thirty years— I don't need you doing it for me."

The muscles clenched in his jaw. "If you really mean that, I'll go," he said, each word like a shard of ice. "And I won't be back. Ever."

Blank shock replaced the fury in Marcia's face; her cheeks were as pale as the wall behind her. But Quentin had gone too far to back off. In a voice like a steel blade he said, "Love's not just good times, Marcia—baby-sitting and family dinners and movies. It's about crises and accidents and losses as well. It's about us sharing whatever happens, because that way each of us is stronger. You letting me see that you need me...me showing you how much I need you. But if you won't let me near you there's no point."

Although how he would live without her, he couldn't begin to contemplate.

She said incoherently, "That's emotional blackmail, what you're doing to me."

"If that's how you see it, then I'm out of here. For good."

Her face crumpled. She sat down hard on the edge of the tub. "You don't understand—I was responsible for Tansy and she could have been killed. I can't bear it, Quentin, I can't bear it!"

He knelt beside her. Tears were streaming down her face, and he was almost sure the pain in her drowned eyes had very little to do with Tansy. Or even with him. He said urgently, "What can't you bear?"

She let her head fall to his shoulder, her back a long curve of surrender. "My father died when I was only five," she whispered, so softly that he had to strain to hear her. "There was a red-haired boy in my class—Kevin Meade. I hated him. He used to pull my hair, and on rainy days he'd throw my books in the puddles. He told me it was my fault my father died because I'd stolen some apples from Mr. Bates's trees on the way home from school. I knew stealing was wrong, so I believed him—I'd been a bad girl, and that was why my father had died and gone to heaven. It was all my fault."

In his mind's eye he could picture a little dark-haired girl with pigtails, climbing over a fence and plucking a ripe red apple from the tree. "Why didn't you tell your mother?"

"She went somewhere else when Daddy died. I don't mean physically... it was as though she was dead inside. Totally absent. I thought that was my fault too." She looked up, the tip of her nose pink. "I know it sounds silly. But I was only five years old."

"In effect you lost both parents."

Her eyes widened. "You're right—in a way, I did. I couldn't talk to Lucy, she was only three, and Cat was just a baby. So I tried very hard to be good so nothing else awful would happen. Good all the time. I was always top in my class, and I never broke any of the rules anywhere."

Quentin was beginning to think that he owed brainless Tansy a debt of gratitude, because Marcia had just given him the key to understanding her. "I think it's called control," he said.

She wiped her nose with the back of her hand. "I became a doctor, of course. Except for Lucy our whole family is nothing but doctors—and even she married one. I did everything right. Medals and scholarships all through university, research papers that attracted a lot of attention, guest speaker at important conferences. It wasn't until Michael died and I met you that I began to realize how unhappy I was. How empty. When I saw that painting of yours at the exhibition it was everything I've never allowed myself to be. I felt as though you knew me."

"No wonder you cried."

"Like a rainy day in April." She sagged against him, rubbing her cheek against his chest. "It's funny, I feel lighter, somehow, now that I've told you."

"Good," Quentin said prosaically, acutely aware of the softness of her breast against his arm.

"I do need you," she blurted. "But what happens if I need you and you're not there?"

"Marcia," he said, as strongly as if it were a vow, "to the best of my ability I'll always be there for you. I swear that."

"I'm going to cry again," she muttered. But as a fresh crop of tears sprang to her lashes she also smiled at him so sweetly that his heart dissolved within him. "Cat's going to be back in an hour or so... and what are you doing here anyway? I thought you were off communing with the lake.''

''When I came back and phoned you and got that damned machine again, I figured I'd come into town.'' He tweaked at her hair. ''I much prefer the real person.''

He got up, flipped the drain shut on the tub and turned on the taps. Then he surveyed the row of bottles on the shelf over the sink, opened one and poured a very generous dollop of pale blue liquid into the tub. Marcia gave a gasp of horror. ''That's Cat's favorite bubble bath—it's horrendously expensive.''

''She owes you,'' he said, and poured in some more.

Marcia giggled. ''You won't be able to find me for bubbles.''

''Try me,'' said Quentin, and reached for the buttons on her shirt.

For the first time since she'd trailed up the front path there was some color in Marcia's cheeks. She sat very still as, one by one, he undid the buttons. His fingers felt clumsy; his heart was pumping as if he'd taken his canoe down a whitewater river. He tugged the shirt free of her waistband, then eased it from her shoulders. Against the white bubbles of the bathtub her skin was palest ivory, as smooth as the silk shirt he had removed. Her bra cupped her breasts; through its white lace he could see the darker circle of her nipples, the tips as hard as the seeds of an apple. He said huskily, ''I'd like to paint you like that—because I don't have words to tell you how beautiful you are.''

Acting on instinct, Marcia lifted her face for his kiss, a long, deep kiss of mouth and tongue, of exploration and entry. His hands were roaming her shoulders, her arms, the hollow at the small of her back. Then his head dropped to her breast, and in a shaft of sweetness she felt the warmth of his face against her flesh. She pressed him to her, playing with his thick black hair, overwhelmed with emotions new to her. True emotions, she thought confusedly. Real ones.

Something cool and wet touched her spine. She glanced down and said, laughter warming her voice, "We're going to have a flood on our hands any minute."

The bubbles were rising over the sides of the tub. Quentin said a very rude word and turned off the taps. She stood up, the twist of her body in her jeans stabbing him with a complex mixture of lust and love. He said thickly, "I'd better get out of here or I'll be making love to you on the bath mat."

He was almost out of the door when she said clearly, "Quentin—thank you."

She was enveloped in a cloud of steam, a small, slim woman wearing jeans and a bra, who meant more to him than anyone he'd ever known. He nodded in acknowledgement, went out to the kitchen and doused her shirt in cold water. He should do the same to himself, he thought wryly, gazing out the window at Cat's tidy front garden.

He was glad Troy had bought Marcia the painting of the three carefree little girls running through the field. She'd lost that freedom much too young, and it had taken her all these years to admit it. Was he deluding himself to think that she would only truly rediscover herself in bed with him?

Half an hour later Cat arrived home. Artie woofed a welcome. Cat hugged her sister briefly and said, "Don't tell me you've broken Tansy of her habit of devouring everyone who comes to the front door."

Marcia said, "Tansy's at the vet's," and described what had happened. Quentin heard the quiver in her voice.

Cat said carelessly, "I'm not surprised. I told you that dog had a screw loose—I can't imagine why Lydia puts up with her."

"You didn't really warn me how badly behaved she is."

"Don't make such a big deal of it, Marcie. I'm glad she's all right—but you needn't blame yourself. Give me the vet bill, though. You shouldn't have to pay that."

Cat didn't have the slightest clue what the episode had meant to her sister—and if she had, would she have cared? Marcia said steadily, "How was New York?"

Cat gave them an enthusiastic description of the plays she had seen and of the exhibitions at the Met. Then Marcia said, "I've got to go, Cat, I'm tired. Glad you had a good time."

"Thanks for everything... I'll treat you to dinner soon at that new place everyone's raving about. Bye, Quentin."

Quentin followed Marcia down the path, carrying her suitcase, angered by Cat's cavalier attitude and amazed that three sisters could be so different.

After he had put the case on the back seat of Marcia's new car he straightened, feeling the wind ruffle his hair, watching it blow dark strands across Marcia's face. There were faint mauve shadows under her eyes. His head was telling him to leave her now, to go back to the cottage and let her digest what had happened, but his gut was saying, Stay—she's exhausted and vulnerable—now's the time to make your move. He said flatly, "You'll be all right, Marcia? I thought I'd head back to the lake."

As her shoulders sagged infinitesimally with relief his jaw clenched. Would the day ever come when she'd want to be with him all the time? Was he a fool to hang around waiting for that day?

"Troy and Lucy want the four of us to go out for dinner on Tuesday," she said. "Would you like to do that?"

Two days before he saw her again. Forty-eight hours. "If that's your best offer."

With a touch of desperation she said, "I'll let you know on Friday whether I'll move in with you at the cottage—I promise I will." Impulsively she reached up and cupped his face, slowly tracing the jut of his cheekbones, the slight bump in his nose, the dark brows and the fan of lines at the corners of his eyes.

It was, he thought, almost as though she were seeing him for the first time. Memorizing him. Wondering if he'd ever be able to anticipate what she would do next, he rasped, "I'm not going to go away."

Her fingertips were clasping the angle of his jaw, her eyes as shy as a wild creature's; she kissed him softly on the lips. Then, bemused, she stepped back. "I'll see you Tuesday. We're meeting at Troy's at seven."

"I'll pick you up at ten to seven."

Her little car pulled away from the curb. Quentin stood there until it was out of sight, then drove back to the cottage, which seemed distressingly empty, and barbecued a steak that could have been made of plastic for all the taste it had.

He didn't want to go canoeing again, and he'd walked everywhere there was to walk. None of the books he picked up seemed to say anything that even remotely connected to the way he was feeling. He pulled a sketchpad towards him and began to draw.

The next morning he replaced the canvas on his easel with a freshly sketched one, smaller than usual, and began to work, cudgeling his brain to remember the photos in Lucy's living room in Vancouver. On Tuesday afternoon, unshaven, his legs and back aching, he knew the painting was finished, and when he drove into the city he took it with him. Carrying it gingerly, because it was still wet, he tapped on Marcia's door.

She was wearing the red dress, gold earrings dangling from her lobes. He swallowed hard, because how could he detach the gift of a painting from the gift of himself? "I did this for you," he said.

Her face lit up like a child's. "A painting? For me?"

"It's wet. Is there somewhere I can prop it up?"

Marcia led him into the living room and moved some ornaments, watching him lean the oil painting against the wall and stand back. In silence she looked at it.

The focus of the work was the figure of a woman in a swirling red dress: herself. The woman was surrounded by a dark background from which emerged the faces of her mother and father, while almost hidden in the shadows was a red-haired boy; lastly, and here Marcia's eyes lingered, in one corner was a little girl who was also herself. Somehow the energy of the painting was such that all the faces were gathered into the lissome curves of the woman's body, inextricably part of her grace and beauty.

Almost inaudibly she said, "Will I ever be that woman, Quentin?"

"I think you already are."

Unconsciously she stood a little taller. "It's the most wonderful gift anyone has ever given me," she said gravely. "You've given me myself—and yourself too." Because—and she had seen this immediately—it was very obvious that the artist was in love with his subject.

She turned to face him, the radiance of her smile taking his breath away. "Your best suit," she remarked. "I'm flattered. And do you know what? Whenever I'm away from you, I can never believe that your eyes are that incredible blue. Gorgeous eyes." Her smile widened. "Sexy eyes... bedroom eyes."

"Dearest Marcia," Quentin said, "you wouldn't be trying to seduce me, would you?"

Flustered, she replied, "I'm out of practise. Heck, who am I kidding? I've never been *in* practise. But I suppose I am."

"I love your technique, but your timing's atrocious—we're supposed to be at Lucy's in precisely five minutes."

She glanced over her shoulder at the painting, in which her dress glowed like a ruby. She said slowly, "You really do love me, don't you, Quentin?"

"I've been trying to convince you of that ever since I met you."

In a low voice she said, "I don't feel worthy of such a gift—and I'm not fishing for compliments and I'm not going to cry because I'll ruin my mascara."

"Look how you've changed in the last three weeks," he said forcibly. "Courage, passion, laughter—you've got them all. They just went underground a long time ago, that's all. Yes, I love you, and when my fingers are too arthritic to hold a paintbrush I'll still love you."

"When you look at me like that," she sputtered, "I want to strip off that very expensive suit you're wearing, not to mention your shirt and tie, and drag you off to the nearest bed."

"Feel free," Quentin said, grasping her under the armpits and lifting her high over his head. He laughed exultantly. "I'm going to enjoy being seduced by you, Dr. Marcia Barnes."

"We'll be late," she said.

"Kiss me," he ordered, lowering her feet to the floor. As she did so, with unabashed delight, his body responded instantly and predictably. "Call Lucy and tell her that it's not food we're interested in eating."

She fluttered her lashes. "I hate to sound unromantic, but I didn't take time for lunch today. How about food first?"

"What's happened since Sunday?" he asked quizzically. "You're different."

She said with a violence that charmed him, "I'm sick to death of playing it safe. Winter's over and I'm tired of being underground... I want to be like those tulips all along the canal, with the sun on my face, and I suppose it's got something to do with telling you about my father. Quentin, we've really got to go. You know Lucy—she'll suspect the worst."

"If I have my way, her suspicions will be well founded as soon as possible," he said.

When they got to the apartment Evelyn was holding the baby, Henry was warming the baby's bottle, and Lucy and Troy were waiting for them—Lucy wearing her purple dress, Troy looking tall and distinguished in a charcoal-gray suit. "Shall we take one car?" Troy asked.

"Two," said Quentin, "so I can drive Marcia home."

Marcia blushed, Lucy looked at them speculatively, and Troy said affably, "Let's go."

The restaurant had a small dance floor and a menu that reduced Marcia to indecision. "I want one of everything," she said. "If I have the baked Brie I could have salmon steak, but if I have smoked salmon I'd go for the rack of lamb. What are you having, Quentin?"

"Fish chowder, if it hasn't got any shrimp in it—I'll check with the waiter. And the loin of pork with mangoes."

They ordered cocktails and Marcia finally settled on Brie and salmon, after which Quentin led her onto the dance floor.

Afterward she couldn't have said whether he was a good or an indifferent dancer, all she was aware of was the closeness of his body and the provocative shift of muscle under the fabric of his suit. As his arm curved possessively around her waist her imagination ran riot.

She wanted the evening to end with him in her bed, this man whose blue eyes spoke to her so ardently of love and desire. Yet the wild excitement this prospect engendered was shot through with flashes of panic.

The music stopped. Quentin took her back to the table and a few minutes later Troy asked her to dance. As he waltzed her expertly round the floor he said, "Looks like Lucy's subjecting Quentin to the third degree."

"Troy," Marcia burst out, "did you know right from the start that Lucy was the woman you wanted?"

"Yep. Although I fought it pretty hard. Just about as hard as you're fighting Quentin."

"I'm thinking of giving up fighting."

"And that scares you, hmm?"

"You're a very nice man and I'm so glad you're my brother-in-law," Marcia said. "You bet it does."

"Quentin's straight, Marcia—he's been an honest and loyal friend to both me and Lucy, and you can't fake that. So if you're asking for advice, I'd say jump in with both feet." He twirled her in a complicated circle. "Love *is* what makes the world go round. Living with Lucy and Chris gives my life its meaning. Go for it, sis." He grinned at her. "By the way, I like you in red—it suits you."

But Marcia hadn't finished. "You and Lucy, you've known each other—what is it, more than six years?— and you both look more in love than you ever were. Will it last, Troy? Can you love one person your whole life through?"

"You sure ask difficult questions," Troy said in an amused voice. "Quentin's got you all stirred up, hasn't he?"

She tripped over his toe. "Quentin and my hormones."

He thought for a moment, steering her between two other couples. Then he said, "If Lucy and I hadn't loved each other with the kind of love that's got a good dose

of determination in it—the determination to last a
lifetime, I mean—I think we'd have stayed apart after
Michael died. We'd have divorced, I suppose.'' He grimaced. ''We came perilously close as it was. But something held us together, which for want of a better word
we called love... I'll love Lucy until the day I die—I
know that in my gut. But I can't explain it in any way
that makes sense.''

''Maybe you don't need to.'' Marcia chewed on her
lip. ''It was when Michael died and you and Lucy separated that I started to realize how sterile my life was.
How empty of love. I'd much rather he'd never died
Troy—but in a way a little bit of good did come out of
it.''

Troy, who was an accomplished dancer, missed a step;
for a moment Marcia saw agony lacerate his features.
Distressed, she said, ''I'm sorry! I should never have
mentioned—''

He picked up the rhythm again and said evenly, ''If
good doesn't come out of bad there's not much point,
is there? And I never want to act as if Michael didn't
exist. I'm glad you told me—thanks.''

She had her answer, Marcia thought. Troy believed in
love that lasted forever and so did Lucy. She'd be willing
to bet that Quentin did too. But what of herself? Was
she capable of that kind of love?

The waltz ended and Troy accompanied her back to
the table. But before they reached the others, he said,
''Good luck, sis—give it the best you've got.''

She braced herself to meet Quentin's inquiring look
and Lucy's smug one, and was relieved to see that the
appetizers had arrived.

They ate and drank, they talked about everything
under the sun and they laughed a lot. Marcia was having
a wonderful time. Her earlier panic had vanished, sub-
limated in the sexual energy that crackled and danced

between her and Quentin in every look they exchanged, in every small touch. When he bent to pick up the napkin she had dropped he said, for her ears alone, "You look like the woman in the painting, sweetheart." And that was indeed how she felt: graceful, sensual, fully alive.

The entrées were delicious, and while they were waiting for the dessert menu Marcia excused herself to go to the washroom and Lucy followed her. The bathroom was very elegant, with gold taps and a spray of orchids in a crystal vase on the marble counter. As Marcia gazed in the gilt-edged mirror at her sparkling eyes and flushed cheeks she scarcely recognized herself.

Lucy took out her lipstick and said, "You look fantastic, Marcie. You should wear bright colors all the time."

"I may do that," said Marcia, running a brush through her hair. She had already checked that they were alone in the bathroom. Gathering her courage, she said, "Lucy, can I ask you something really personal?"

Lucy was frowning at her lower lip, now neatly outlined in red. "Go ahead."

"I don't really... What I want to ask is... I mean, do you really like sex, Lucy? It's more than six years now... is it still okay?" Too embarrassed to meet her sister's eyes, Marcia fumbled in her evening bag for her own lipstick.

Lucy sat down on the marble counter, her lipstick brush in one hand, the tube of lipstick in the other, and gave her answer her full consideration. "It isn't always that dynamite stuff you read about in books," she said thoughtfully. "But you wouldn't want a symphony to play loud all the time either, would you? It can be friendly and playful... or so full of tenderness you think you might die of happiness. And sometimes it's just plain old lust." She gave an unselfconscious giggle.

"Last week we made love up against the kitchen door while I was cooking supper... the carrots burned and the broccoli was soggy and we ended up ordering Chinese food." She was warming to her theme. "It's like anything else—you get what you give. Sometimes when Troy's schedule is exceptionally heavy we'll make a date, and all day we'll know that's what we're going to do when we're alone together... those times are wonderful. But, you see, we love and trust each other too, Marcia, and we're committed to each other—so there's always that running through it." She swirled the brush in the lipstick. "I'm talking too much. Is that any help?"

"I... guess so."

"Sometimes you just have to jump in at the deep end," Lucy announced.

"Take the plunge," Marcia riposted, smiling at her sister's reflection.

"Take the risk," Lucy said, sounding very fierce. "I learned that in the year Troy and I were apart. Don't push Quentin away because you're afraid, Marcie, that's the worst thing you could do—and now I really will shut up. Troy's always telling me I interfere too much." She filled in the rest of her lips and said casually, "My hair's a disaster—I must get it cut. Shall we go?"

But when they went back to their table Troy was sitting there alone. He pulled back Lucy's chair and said evenly, "They changed chefs this evening unexpectedly, so the waiter didn't know that the chowder had a shrimp broth in it—Quentin just left; he was feeling lousy. He knows the symptoms by now and he said he'd be all right... He sent his apologies and asked if I'd drive you home, Marcia."

"Was he going back to the cottage?" Marcia asked in dismay.

"Yeah... I tried to persuade him to go to our apartment, but no dice."

"How long ago did he leave?" she flashed.

"A couple of minutes before you came back. He said it always hits him like a ton of bricks . . . Where are you off to?"

Clutching her evening bag, Marcia was already halfway round the table. "I'll see if I can catch him in the car park. He should go to my place, not all the way to the cottage. If I'm too late, I'll be back in a minute."

She dashed between the tables, grabbed her jacket from the rack and ran outside into the warm spring evening.

CHAPTER TEN

QUENTIN had parked in an underground lot across the street. Marcia checked for traffic and sprinted across the road. There was a young man with a Vandyke beard in the booth. "Excuse me," she said breathlessly, "has a man in a yellow sportscar just left?"

"No, ma'am. No one's left in the last fifteen minutes."

"This is the only exit?"

"Yes, ma'am."

She'd wait here, then, she thought, ignoring his curious look, and heard the roar of an approaching motor. Blinded by the headlights, she stood to one side and saw that it was Quentin's car. As he drew up at the barrier and rolled down his window she took the ticket from him, thrust a five-dollar bill at the attendant and said, "Move over, Quentin—we're going to my place."

He looked ghastly—his features drained of color, his forehead beaded with sweat. "I'm not inflicting—"

"Or else I'll go to the cottage with you."

The attendant was trying to give her the change. She grabbed it and said impatiently, "Which is it to be?"

Quentin's fingers tightened on the wheel and his face contracted with pain. When he could speak, he said, "I'm better off alone. I don't want you—"

"This is about you needing me," she interrupted furiously.

"I never let anyone—"

"Our whole relationship has been about change," she cried, with no idea where the words were coming from. "You've got to change too! Because need works both

133

ways—it has to." She gave him a sudden rueful smile. "And I am a doctor, Quentin. In case you'd forgotten."

He swiped at his forehead and didn't smile back. "Why don't you get lost?"

Her lashes flickered. "No."

"Then get in, for God's sake," he snarled, clambering over the clutch and collapsing in the passenger seat.

Remembering to throw a smile of thanks at the attendant, Marcia opened the door, sat in the driver's seat and quickly checked the unfamiliar pedals. Quentin said nastily, "You win—how does it feel?"

His eyes were like chips of ice. She said, "If you hate me for winning, we both lose."

"Very clever," he sneered.

She eased out the clutch and managed to get up the incline without stalling. "You're just as bad as I am," she snapped. "About letting people close to you."

"I'm a man. It's different."

"Oh, sure. What are the skeletons in your closet, Quentin?"

Jerkily he wrapped his arms around his belly and hunched over in the seat. "Just get me to your place, will you?"

Quickly Marcia planned the shortest route to her condo; she drove as fast as was safe and whipped through two yellow lights. And all the while, despite the fact that she was almost certain Quentin would rather have been on his own, she knew that she was exactly where she wanted to be. So much for detachment, she thought, sneaking a sideways glance at her companion.

He was leaning back in the seat, his eyes closed; one hand was wrapped around the seat belt strap, the knuckles white with strain. "Two more blocks," she said in a neutral voice. "Tell me what to expect."

"I get these godawful cramps," he muttered. "Then I'll spend the better part of the night vomiting everything I've eaten for the last four days. No fun."

She parked on the street in front of her building and got out, locking the car. When she walked round to Quentin's side he was trying to stand upright. He staggered a little and she seized him by the arm, knowing that if he fell she'd never be able to get him to his feet. "Sorry, Doc," he said sarcastically, "I forgot to tell you about the dizziness."

"Let's go."

Fortunately there were only three steps to the lobby and they had the elevator to themselves. By the time they reached her door, Quentin was leaning most of his weight on her; she unlocked it and almost pushed him inside. He headed straight for the bathroom, closing the door behind him. She hung up her jacket and went into her bedroom, where she changed into leggings and a loose green sweatshirt and changed the sheets on the bed. Then she walked down the hall to the bathroom.

From inside she could hear Quentin retching; she clutched the doorframe, feeling utterly helpless and as miserable as though his suffering were her own. She paced up and down the hallway for fifteen minutes, then made herself a cup of coffee and poured it down the sink because she didn't feel like drinking it, and finally went back to the bathroom door. She heard only silence from within—a dead, waiting silence; in sudden terror she called Quentin's name.

As though he were in the next condo rather than on the other side of the door, he said, "Don't fuss—I'm fine."

He didn't sound fine. He sounded horribly weak. Marcia tried the doorhandle and found it locked. In a surge of anger she said, "Quentin, let me in."

"I'll be in here for hours and there's nothing you can do... You might as well go back to the restaurant."

"And leave you alone?" she cried.

"I can look after myself."

It was an uncanny echo of her own words two days ago. I've looked after myself for over thirty years, she had told Quentin, and as a result he had threatened to leave her. Forever. That works two ways, she thought vengefully. "Cut out the macho stuff and unlock the door," she stormed, rattling the handle.

With a suddenness that took her by surprise the handle turned. As she stumbled inside Quentin was standing in the opening, leaning heavily on the door, his face with the hard pallor of marble. "Go away, Marcia. I haven't got the energy for arguing."

He looked terrible, and for a moment her anger faltered. But in some obscure way she knew that she was fighting for something vital to both of them. "I'm a doctor," she said shortly, "I'm not going to pass out if you look less than perfect. Plus I'm the woman you say you want to spend the rest of your life with. Is that just the good days, Quentin? Or is it your whole life, good and bad—the days when you're healthy and the days when you're sick as a dog?"

"I'm a doctor" seemed to be becoming a refrain in her life, she thought wildly, and waited for him to answer.

"There's not a goddamned thing you can do—will you get that through your thick head?"

Although she flinched from the anger in his voice, she stood her ground. "I can be with you," she said.

His throat felt like sandpaper and there was a vise squeezing his belly, making him dizzy and sick. But through the pain he could see a kind of stubborn courage superimposed on Marcia's delicate features. "You don't know when to give up, do you?"

She didn't think he meant that as a compliment. "Do you want me to?"

"That seems like one hell of a complicated question," he said muzzily. Then his face changed. "Vamoose."

She did as she was told. But when the horrible bout of sickness had ended she went back into the bathroom. He was sitting on the edge of the tub, his head in his hands. His hair, she saw with a pang of compassion, was wet with sweat and he was shivering. She went into her bedroom and came back with a multi-hued mohair sweater she had knitted a couple of years ago, draping it over his shoulder.

He turned his head into its soft folds. "It smells of your perfume... You made one like it for Lucy, didn't you? She had it with her on Shag Island."

She nodded, stroking his hair back from his forehead and trying to warm him with her body. He didn't push her away but he didn't hold her close either, and somehow she wasn't surprised when he muttered, "So much for our romantic evening."

"Quentin," Marcia said emphatically, "if you still want to, we'll make love. Not tonight, that's for sure. But soon. I'm just sorry you're feeling so awful, and that's got nothing to do with making love."

He looked up, his eyes sunk deep in their sockets. "If I still want to? I can't imagine that I'll ever stop wanting to. How could I, when I love you as much as I do?"

She was certain he was in no state to speak anything but the truth. So he was offering her the kind of love of which Troy had spoken, she thought in awe, and said shakily, "Why do some of our most intimate moments take place in the bathroom?"

"When I get my strength back, I'll remedy that."

"The bedroom would be a distinct improvement," she teased. "In the meantime I want you to drink something so you don't get dehydrated. I'll be right back."

The night wore on, the bouts of sickness gradually spacing themselves farther and farther apart, until finally she heard Quentin splashing water on his face and gargling with mouthwash. He walked out into the hall, leaning one hand on the wall. "At the risk of losing whatever remains of my macho image, I don't think I'm safe to drive home," he said. "Can I bunk down on your couch until tomorrow?"

"No," she said with a big smile, infinitely relieved to know that the ordeal was over, "you can bunk down in my bed. I'll take the couch."

"Marcia..." She looked pale and tired; it was three in the morning and he knew she hadn't slept at all. "Thanks," he said gruffly. "It was sweet of you to take such good care of me."

"Just obeying the Hippocratic oath," she said fliply.

Like a shadow, an indefinable emotion passed over his face, and she heard the words replay in her mind. She rested her palm on his chest and said, "Sorry, Quentin—that was the old Marcia speaking, wasn't it? The keep-you-at-arm's-length-at-any-cost Marcia. Hippocrates would have fired me tonight—I definitely did not maintain the proper attitude of medical detachment from my patient. Come and lie down before you fall down."

She had a three-quarter mahogany bed that had belonged to her great-grandfather, a thoracic surgeon. Her walls were painted ivory while the drapes and bedspread were softly patterned in spring flowers. It was a restful room, now lit only by a bedside lamp. For a moment Quentin looked around him; somehow he had expected something more stark, less welcoming. Then, to his enormous gratification, he saw that she had moved his painting of the woman in the red dress to her bureau, where she could see it from her bed.

Marcia said nervously, "You're the first man who's ever been in here."

Because his knees were giving out he sat down on the edge of the bed; his head was pounding and he felt very cold. "I trust I'll be the last," he said, watching her lashes lower to hide her eyes. Without finesse he added, "Sleep with me, Marcia."

Startled, she looked up. "I—I'd disturb you when I get up in the morning."

"After one of these sessions, it'd take a bulldozer to disturb me." His smile was twisted. "And sleep's all I'm capable of—this ain't no proposition, honey."

Blushing, she stammered, "Well, I—I guess so. If you—I mean, if you're sure that's what you want."

He loved it when she lost her cool. "What I want, I can't deliver. Not—" He broke off as he was seized by a violent fit of shivering; gritting his teeth, he fought to control it.

"Oh, Quentin, I'm a lousy doctor—just look at you," she cried, and started undoing the buttons on his shirt, her fingers awkward with emotion and haste.

He said thickly, "This isn't quite the way I pictured being in your bedroom."

Her hands stilled. With that rare, sweet smile that always smote him to the core, she said, "Nor I. But I wouldn't want you to be anywhere else."

His cufflinks were intricate and her fingers all thumbs, but finally she tugged his shirt from his body. After she'd undone his belt buckle and taken off his socks he managed to get to his feet again. Her tongue caught between her teeth, she fumbled with the zipper on his trousers. He said roughly, "You're the first woman I've ever allowed to look after me like this."

She gave him a faint ironical smile. "I have no difficulty believing that."

"A very different kind of intimacy than I'd planned."

"Is that why you were less than happy to see me when I turned up at the car park?"

"Yeah ... sorry about that. I learned to be self-sufficient pretty young."

As his trousers slid to the carpet in a heap she said wryly, "So while you have grounds to fire me as a doctor, you won't fire me as a woman?"

"Full employment guaranteed." With a relief he couldn't hide, Quentin sank down on the mattress and hauled the covers up over his chest. "Which side do you sleep on?"

His lean hips and long, muscled legs had filled her with an agony of longing. "The middle, actually."

He rolled over until he was in the center of the bed. "Your sheets are like ice—hurry up and get in bed."

He sounded more like a husband of several years than an ardent lover, she thought. Whereas she felt like a timorous virgin. Grabbing her nightgown from under her pillow, she fled to the bathroom. But when she came back a few minutes later, Quentin was still awake.

She had bought her nightgown in the lingerie shop. It was made of thin flowered silk, with narrow straps and a loosely draped bodice that revealed the shadowed cleavage between her breasts; the fabric clung at waist and hip and thigh. For a moment Marcia hesitated in the doorway, for she'd been hoping he'd be asleep. But when she saw how his eyes flew to meet hers, as though she were his lodestar, she was suddenly glad that he had stayed awake.

With unselfconscious grace she hung up her red dress in the closet, then sat down at her dressing table and removed her earrings and bracelet. She then smoothed off her make-up and brushed her hair, all her movements unhurried.

Quentin lay still. Because he had no physical reserves to draw on, all his emotions were so close to the surface that he felt naked and exposed. When Marcia walked over to the bed and reached for the switch on the lamp, the light shone through her nightgown, delineating the curves of her body; through the throbbing in his temples he knew he was bound to her for as long as he lived. Then darkness fell and he heard the small sounds as she slid into bed beside him.

He reached over and pulled her to him. She gasped, "You're freezing!"

"I love you," Quentin said jaggedly.

Marcia rested her head on his shoulder and wrapped one arm round his chest, her breasts soft against his ribcage. "I don't think I'm ready for that word yet," she whispered, "but I've never felt with anyone else the way I feel with you, Quentin. I want you to know that." As she eased one thigh over his, trying to warm him, she added with a throaty chuckle, "This is so weird— almost as though we've been married for years."

"It's bloody marvelous," said Quentin, and closed his eyes.

Within seconds his breathing had deepened and he was asleep. Intending to savor the intimate closeness of his body in her bed, the gradual warming of his flesh, Marcia closed her eyes...and when she opened them her bedside clock informed her that she was fifty minutes late for work.

Quentin was deeply asleep, curled into her back, his breath cool against her shoulderblade. She didn't want to get up. She wanted to stay here all day, in bed with Quentin, and see what happened when he woke up. Stealthily she edged away from him. He flopped over on his back, his hair black against her pillow, his big body taking up most of the mattress. We'll need a queen-sized bed, she thought, and with a small shock of surprise wondered if her decision wasn't already made.

Half an hour later, showered and dressed and chewing on a muffin, Marcia hurried out the door. She was reluctant to leave Quentin—although "reluctant" was scarcely an adequate word to describe the wrench of frustration as she locked the door behind her—but she was also reluctant to go to the lab in a way that was new to her. While she could usually immerse herself in her work to the exclusion of all else, the last two days had been nothing but rumors and counter-rumors about cutbacks and layoffs—the staff tense and edgy, the management staying well out of the way. Today she'd shut herself in her office and edit the paper she was to present at a conference in Brussels in September, she decided as she pulled out into the street.

Unfortunately she couldn't altogether shut out the world. Her secretary had heard that fifty percent of the junior research staff were to lose their jobs, the co-author of one of Marcia's papers had it on good authority that there would be no layoffs at all and one of the janitors confided that his wife was sick and he couldn't afford to lose his job. It was no atmosphere in which to work, although Marcia did her best.

But at three in the afternoon she found herself gazing out the window of her office, her paper only half edited, her pencil idle. Fifty percent of the junior staff might include herself.

Her job was her life. She couldn't lose it.

Quentin, she thought. I'll go home to Quentin. I don't have to tell him what's going on. But if I'm with him, at least I won't be churning it over and over in my mind.

Her decision made, emotions washed over her as turbulent as the rapids on the Ottawa River. The rumors, upsetting though they were, really had very little to do with her inability to concentrate. All day, she thought, she had been worrying about Quentin, wanting to be home with him, wondering if he was feeling better.

Wondering if he still wanted to make love to her.

She pushed her papers in her drawer, shucked off her lab coat, threw her sweater over her shoulders and, with the air of a woman on very important business, ran out to her car. Fifteen minutes later she was unlocking the door of her condo.

Quentin was singing, loudly and unmelodiously, over the splash of water in the bathroom. Marcia closed the door behind her, a silly grin on her face, and called his name. He didn't hear her. She walked down the hall to the open bathroom door and stood there, her eyes meeting his in the mirror, her smile wider. He broke off his song in mid-bar. He had just finished shaving. He was wearing a pink towel swathed around his hips, and nothing else. Marcia said, strolling in the door, "You're a better artist than a singer."

"I'm dreaming," he said, his blue eyes blazing with such happiness at her appearance that her heart began to race. "Or else you're home early."

"You're wide awake, and here we are in the bathroom again."

"So we are." He dabbed at a cut on his chin. "Your razor is entirely inadequate for my beard, my love, and I haven't any clean clothes."

"Then maybe you should go back to bed."

"Only if you'll join me... After all, you were up half the night."

She pursed her lips. "Are you trying to tell me I don't look so hot?"

"You look extremely beautiful—although that skirt and top should be consigned to the back of your closet."

The skirt was brown, the top beige. "I spent enough money the other day without revamping my entire wardrobe, Quentin Ramsey. You must be feeling better—you're starting to complain again."

He rinsed off her pink plastic razor and turned to face her. "I slept the clock round—I feel wonderful. And I wasn't expecting you for another three hours."

"I couldn't concentrate."

"Because you were tired?"

"No, that wasn't the reason."

"Because it's really spring and the sun is shining?"

Take the risk... wasn't that what Lucy had said? "Because I wanted to be here with you," Marcia said.

He walked up to her, put his arms around her and kissed her. Her palms against his bare chest, aware of his nakedness with every nerve in her body, Marcia kissed him back, and with her mouth expressed the seesaw of emotions she had gone through in the last twenty-four hours—all the fear, compassion, tenderness and longing. As he covered her face with tiny kisses she tangled her fingers in his body hair. "You smell nice."

He laughed. "Your soap was a little too feminine for me—I don't think I'm the lily of the valley type. So I swiped your herbal shampoo and showered with that."

She nibbled gently at his shoulder. "The results are splendiferous."

"You have," he said huskily, "a wonderful way with words. You also have far too many clothes on."

He pushed her sweater from her shoulders, then pulled her short-sleeved knit top over her head. As he undid the zipper her brown skirt fell to her feet, and quickly she stepped out of her hose. Under her very ordinary work clothes she was wearing her raspberry-red lingerie. Quentin raised his brows. "You're full of surprises," he said, his eyes darkening as he took her breasts in his hands and teased their tips beneath the delicate lace.

She swayed toward him, parting her lips for his kiss, feeling their tongues entwined. As he clasped her by the hips, pulling her against a hardness that was both hunger and need, the towel slithered down to join the heap of clothes on the floor. Marcia ran her hand down his back, holding him by the jut of his pelvic bone, feeling the muscles tighten as he thrust himself between her legs. Heat enveloped her like fire. She threw back her head, frantic to join with him. He undid the clasp of her bra, the garment sliding down her body like flame; his tongue encircling her nipple made her shudder with desire.

For a moment Quentin raised his head, his gaze caressing her drowned features, her mouth so soft and seductive a curve from his kisses. Through the pounding of his heart and his own urgency, an urgency beyond anything he'd ever known, he said, "Don't you think it's time we moved our relationship from the bathroom to the bedroom?"

With overt sensuality Marcia drew her fingernails up his back, following the length of his spine, and spoke the literal truth. "I'm not sure I can walk that far."

"That's easily remedied," Quentin said, bending to pick her up.

She looped her arms around his neck, touching one fingertip to the cut on his chin. "We'll have to buy you a proper razor."

"We'll have to buy you one too—I ruined yours." His voice deepened as he walked into her bedroom. "But we can do that later. Right now I have more important things on my mind."

She traced his top lip, admiring its strongly carved line, letting her finger come to rest in the little indentation below his nostrils. "Your nose has character," she said.

"It got broken in a fight when I was thirteen," he said, a fleeting shadow crossing his face. "It didn't set quite straight." Then he smiled down at her with such love in his face that Marcia forgot about his nose. "You wouldn't be attempting to distract me from the matter at hand, would you, my darling?"

"Oh, no," she answered fervently.

So he was laughing as he lowered her to the bed and covered her with the heat and weight of his body. With one hand he drew her last garment from her hips. She wriggled her legs free, feeling the rasp of hair on his thighs, watching his face convulse as she circled her hips slowly and suggestively beneath him. He muttered, "I'll look after contraception—you're driving me out of my mind doing that."

"Good," she said, and, raising herself on her elbows, brushed her breasts against the hard wall of his chest.

He dropped his head and licked the soft swell of her flesh, his tongue moving with such slow, deliberate sensuality that Marcia shuddered with pleasure, her throat stretched taut, her dark hair splayed on the pillow. As if time had stopped, she saw his curls black against the white of her skin, and felt the thrust of his erection against her inner thighs. How would she ever forget this moment? Or this man, who called her to a wildness that she had never suspected was hers?

When her breasts were aching and swollen Quentin moved down her body, parting her thighs and with his fingers gently playing with the petals of flesh between them. Sensation rippled through her, wave after wave, until she was almost sobbing his name. Then he stopped, so suddenly that she moaned in protest. He smothered her moan with another fierce kiss, rolling over and pulling her on top of him.

Marcia clung to him, panting for breath, her irises the dark purple of a sky at nightfall, her body throbbing with primitive, unfulfilled hunger. Slowly she raised her head. The blue depths of Quentin's eyes that she had so feared in her dreams were no longer frightening; the swirling currents of her sexuality had been liberated for her by this man lying beneath her, so loving, passionate and vulnerable.

She knelt over him, beginning her own slow exploration, laying her cheek to his chest, where his heartbeat vibrated like an ancient drum, letting her hands wander over the arch of his ribs and the concavity of his belly to his navel, where the dark hair funneled still lower.

Then, against her palm, she felt the silken smoothness of skin over a hardness like bone, and heard his harsh intake of breath. In a broken voice she would never have recognized as her own, she cried, "Quentin . . . I want you inside me."

He fumbled with the envelope on her bedside table; frantic with haste, she helped him as best she could. He kissed her again, a kiss as possessive as if he were setting his seal on her, the thrust of his tongue matched by the thrusting of his body. She opened to him, lifting her hips and feeling him slide within her as though they had been made for each other. I am both possessed and possessor, she thought distantly, and then abandoned thought for pure sensation, shaft after shaft of brilliant sensation, lancing through her whole frame until they joined into a dazzling brightness like that of sunlight dancing on water.

Deep inside her body she felt Quentin find his own throbbing release. He called her name hoarsely—once, twice. Then he collapsed on top of her, his chest heaving, his forehead falling to her shoulder. She held him close, kissing his hair, filled with a deep, all-encompassing happiness.

When he eventually looked up Quentin had no idea how much time had passed; it could have been seconds or minutes or even hours. He stroked Marcia's hair back from her face and said unsteadily, "From the very first time I saw you I suspected you were a passionate woman, and today you proved me right—you wanted me as much as I wanted you, didn't you, sweetheart? Do you have any idea how wonderful that makes me feel?"

"You can't possibly feel as wonderful as I do right now," Marcia murmured, stretching as luxuriantly as a cat.

"Watch it," he growled, "or you're going to get yourself in trouble."

"You mean I didn't satisfy you?" she asked, big-eyed.

"Witch—you know damn well you satisfied me. Which isn't to say I couldn't be tempted to do it all over again."

Her cheeks were flushed, her eyes very bright, and now that he had possessed her Quentin realized that somewhere deep down he had doubted that he ever would. Even now, he thought, and despite a lovemaking that had been as tempestuous as a spring storm, there was still something missing. In that same deep place he had hoped that in the heat of lovemaking Marcia would tell him that she loved him. She'd been generous and passionate beyond his imagining, but she hadn't spoken those three magical words—I love you.

So neither had he.

He lifted his weight from her, his gaze lingering on the pale slopes and valleys of her body that had been her gift to him. One woman's body; how could it hold so much of rapture and of promise? He said softly, "I'd like to paint you like that."

She blushed delightfully. "Not for that gallery owner to get her hands on."

"No. For us. We could hang it in our bedroom."

She could have said, What bedroom? She could have said, Don't make assumptions, Quentin. She could have said, I'm not sure I love you. Not like Lucy loves Troy. She said none of these. Instead she said, "Do you know what I'd like? An almond croissant from the little bakery down the road."

There was no need to feel frightened, Quentin told himself. Three weeks ago he hadn't even met Marcia, and not everyone fell in love at first sight, as he had. "Not sure a croissant will do it for me—I haven't had anything to eat yet today."

She sat up, her face full of concern. "Oh, Quentin, you must be starving... I wonder what I've got in the freezer."

"I'll take you out for dinner."

"Only if you promise to stick to steak," she said drily.

"And if you'll wear your red dress."

"I'll have to go shopping again; you'll be getting tired of it."

"That's not very likely," said Quentin, and kissed her.

They wandered hand in hand to the bakery and ate croissants with hot chocolate. Then they went to the drugstore to buy Quentin a razor and some soap, and to a men's store where he bought himself some casual clothes.

They then went back to the condo to change for dinner, in the midst of which they made love in an ardent and intent silence. Marcia fell asleep afterward. When she woke, she was alone in her bed; she could hear Quentin moving around in the kitchen, and a delicious smell of curry wafted down the hall.

She lay still, and could acknowledge to herself, now that she was alone, that underlying her happiness she was afraid. Oddly, she felt as though she'd lost her virginity today. Nothing she had ever done had prepared her for an intimacy so total and so impassioned, so altogether undeniable, so much like a force of nature. I can't go back to the way I was, she thought. I'll never be the same again.

He's changed me. Whether I was ready to be changed or not.

CHAPTER ELEVEN

THE next day Marcia was only half an hour late for work. She sneaked into the building by the side door again, certain that one look at her face would tell all her co-workers exactly what she had been doing since they'd seen her last.

But the staff had other things to talk about; management had had a four-hour meeting the day before, and the rumors were as varied as they were unsettling. Marcia plugged away at her paper with her door closed; that way if she found herself gazing at the wall with a silly smile on her face, or blushing at images that had a tendency to pop out of nowhere and that bordered on obscenity, no one could see her.

At four o'clock she entered the last change on her computer, and by four-thirty she was climbing the stairs to her condo. She had left Quentin with a key so he could come and go as he pleased through the day. Hoping he was home, she opened the door, stepped inside and gave an audible gasp of surprise.

The hallway was festooned with wide strips of paper that had been taped to the walls. The paper was covered with charcoal sketches, drawn with an irresistible energy and vitality, of a man and a woman making love. Herself and Quentin.

Marcia walked slowly toward the kitchen, looking from left to right, her cheeks scarlet because Quentin had not censored any of their activities and there was a great deal of bare flesh. Her mouth curved in a smile that, as he came out of the living room, turned into helpless laughter.

"What if I'd brought the chief of police home with me?" she gurgled. "We'd be spending the night in the clink."

Quentin grinned. "I was arrogant enough to think you'd want me to yourself."

"Oh, I do, I do. But Lucy could have dropped in...or my mother and Henry."

"I wouldn't have let them past the door."

Marcia's eyes had been busy. In the sketch next to the living room door she was stretched out on the bed in languorous abandon, her body a series of graceful curves from shoulder to ankle: a portrait of a woman well loved. "I'm not that pretty."

"You haven't looked in the mirror lately."

Her gaze flicked to the opposite wall where, between the doors to the kitchen and the bathroom, she was depicted in a particularly compromising position. "Oh, my goodness, did I really do that?" she said, pressing her hands to her red cheeks and then answering her own question. "Yes, I did, and I loved every minute of it. If you ever decide you're tired of being an artist, you could go into the wallpapering business—you'd revolutionize it. Oh, Quentin, what am I going to *do* with you?"

"Marry me," he said.

"*What*?"

"You heard. Marry me."

She said spiritedly, "The last I heard, you wanted me to move in with you. At the cottage."

"If that's all I wanted, I was fooling myself as well as you. Yes, I want to live with you. Here, or at the cottage, or in Vancouver—the location doesn't matter. But as my wife, Marcia."

The laughter had faded from her face. "I told you I'd give you my answer on Friday."

Quentin tried to tamp down his anger. "Today's Thursday. What's going to change by tomorrow?"

"How do I know? Change seems to follow in your wake. Anything could have happened by then."

"You love me. I know you do."

His certainty for some reason infuriated her. "Then you know more than I do," she said coldly.

As though they had been recorded on tape, she heard her words play back to her—words spoken in anger. Suddenly she stamped her foot. "I hate this! I don't want us to argue." Her voice shook. "I just want to be in bed with you, that's all."

He hardened his heart against the stubborn curve of her jaw and the appeal in her eyes. "I love you," he said. "I'm not going to pretend that I don't."

Unexpectedly her lips quirked. She looked up and down the length of the hall and said with a tiny chuckle, "I'm glad you told me—because I never would have guessed."

Her anger had ignited his own; her laughter defeated him. He gathered her into his arms, kissed her thoroughly to their mutual satisfaction, and steered her into the bathroom. "I bought you a bottle of the same kind of bubble bath that Cat had—want to try it out?"

With the sense that something momentous had been averted, Marcia said, "That was sweet of you, Quentin."

He had put a big spray of larkspur and delphiniums in the corner of the bathroom, and a pile of fluffy purple towels by the tub. As it was filling with hot water he started undressing her. "How did work go today?" he asked, undoing the buttons of her new silk shirt. "You're home early again—you're ruining your reputation as a workaholic."

Knowing she was going to keep the rumors and tensions at the institute to herself, Marcia said, "I finished editing the Brussels paper. I've got another one to do, but I decided I'd start it tomorrow rather than today." As his hands brushed her bare breasts she added impetuously, "All day I've wanted to be home with you, and I'm not sure my bathtub's big enough for two."

"We'll manage," Quentin said, with a note in his voice that she already recognized and that set her heart racing as if she'd run all the way home.

When they were both naked, Quentin sank down into the froth of bubbles and pulled her down on top of him. As she lay back, her head tucked under his chin, the water rose alarmingly high. "There's an overflow valve— I checked," Quentin said, and began stroking the wet peaks of her breasts.

Content to surrender to his touch, Marcia closed her eyes, feeling desire uncurl within her and spread through her whole body until she was nothing but desire, her low moans of pleasure interspersed with the water's soft lapping against her skin. When his hand slid between her thighs, the bittersweet ache of desire became naked hunger, strong and hot and imperative; whimpering, she moved her hips to his skillful, tormenting fingers, until with a cry torn from her throat she was seized by the compelling rhythms of release.

Quentin could feel the frantic racing of her heart against his arm; her breasts rose and fell with her agitated breathing. He kissed her ear, murmuring little love words to her as gradually she quietened. Then she whispered, "Each time I'm with you I feel as though it's the first time I've ever made love."

Touched, he wrapped his arms around her. "You're getting cold; we'd better get out."

She scrambled out of the tub, then gave him her hand to help him out. When they'd dried each other Marcia led the way to her bedroom, his hand still clasped in hers. In the doorway she stopped dead. The room was a bower of flowers—chrysanthemums, snapdragons, roses, cosmos and daisies. At some point Quentin had run out of vases, so some of the flowers were in plastic ice cream containers; the overall effect was of an exuberant and colorful muddle.

She turned to face him, her eyes dancing. "You're a crazy, wonderful man, you know that?"

"I'm the kid who grew up in rural New Brunswick, where we had frosts in June and September. So every time I go near the market and see all those flowers, I want to buy the lot."

She looked around the bedroom again; her bed seemed to have shrunk, surrounded as it was by blossoms. "I think you're close to achieving your aim," she said solemnly. "You could add interior decorating as a sideline to the wallpapering business." Then she looped her arms around his waist, her voice suddenly trembling with intensity. "You make me feel so cherished. And you're so beautiful to me, Quentin—the feel of your muscles, the warmth of your skin, the smell of you... Make love to me. Now."

Her body was trembling too, in a way that inflamed him. He said unsteadily, "Nakedness, so I'm discovering, has almost nothing to do with clothes... Tell me how I can please you, dearest Marcia."

She drew his head to her breast. "This... and this. Anything and everything... Oh, God, Quentin, can one faint from pleasure? Die from it?"

"Let's find out," he said, and lifted her to the bed.

Whether it was the profusion of flowers in all their vivid hues, or her growing trust and familiarity with this man who was her lover, Marcia felt freer than she had ever felt in her life: free to experiment, free to ask Quentin what he wanted and then to do it for him, free to cry out with wanton pleasure and laugh with sheer, voluptuous delight. Their climax had all the tumult of ocean waves on a deserted shore—a deep drowning and a slow, eventual surfacing to the separation that was reality.

Clutching Quentin by the shoulder, because she didn't want to be separate from him, Marcia said faintly, "How can an act of the body ravish the soul?"

He had both ravished her and been ravished by her. He said, speaking the simple truth, "Because we're soulmates."

"My life will never be the same."

"You think mine will?"

Her eyes were downcast, as if she was afraid of where her words had taken her. She licked the saltiness of sweat from his shoulder, tugging gently at his chest hair with her fingers; her lips were swollen from his kisses. "I love your body," she said.

I love you, Quentin wanted to say, but said evenly, "Body and soul—they come together. Package deal."

Her nostrils flared. "You don't let up, do you?"

"I can as easily stop loving you as stop breathing." He cupped the rise of her hip in one palm and said more temperately, "Marcia, we're not going to fight. Not now. For one thing, I don't have the energy." He glanced down at his arm, where he could see the faint parallel marks her fingernails had left, and recalled in graphic detail the precise moment she had done it. "I feel as if I've been in bed with a tiger."

She blushed. "I didn't mean to hurt you."

"I wasn't complaining."

"I should hope not," Marcia responded with a demureness that ill-matched her pink cheeks and her nudity.

Amused, Quentin said, "You're a very vocal lover."

"I never used to be." She gaped at him. "There was nothing much to say."

"I can't imagine you and I suffering from that particular deficit."

Neither could Marcia. So what was stopping her from telling Quentin that she loved him? And how was one more day going to change that?

An hour or so later, Marcia and Quentin went out for dinner. Marcia wore her red dress and Quentin his very expensive suit, and they went to a chic French restaurant whose chef personally assured them that nothing Quentin chose from the menu had come within ten feet of a shrimp. Afterward they walked home, went straight to sleep and made love at dawn. Marcia was late for work again.

Her secretary, a rather flighty young woman called Rosemary, said, "The director wants to see you at two, in his office."

Her curiosity was ill-concealed. Marcia swallowed a flutter of fear and said easily, "Thanks, Rosemary. Any mail?" She then went into her office and turned on her computer. Why would the director want to see her on a Friday afternoon?

By lunchtime she'd found out that three others of the junior staff also had appointments, after hers; this didn't make her feel any better. She could have phoned Quentin. She didn't.

She slogged through her paper, checking her data and redesigning a couple of the tables, and promptly at two presented herself at the door of the director's office.

Dr. Wayne Martell was overweight and ruthlessly efficient; Marcia respected him without liking him very much. "Marcia," he said, closing the door behind her. "Sit down, please."

Outwardly composed, she did as he asked, folding her hands in her lap. He sat down heavily in his swivel chair. "You will, I'm sure, have heard the rumors of financial cutbacks," he said. "Unfortunately they're true. Our budget has been drastically reduced, and myself and the board have come to the conclusion that we have to lay off a number of staff members. We do this, as I hope you will understand, with deep regret and only out of the direst necessity." He paused, fiddling with his gold cufflinks; she had never realized before what a plummy voice he had.

"As you are aware," he went on, "you joined us seven years ago, which places you in the junior category—and it is that category which must be reduced. The institute will suffer from the loss of your extremely valuable contributions to our research program. We only trust that you yourself will not suffer."

He paused, looking at her expectantly. He wants applause, she thought wildly. Admirable job, Dr. Martell. You should fire people more often. She said, without visible emotion, "Are you telling me I no longer have a job here?"

"As of the middle of the month. You will, of course, receive full benefits up until that time."

Thanks a lot, she thought, and struggled to find some dignified way to get out of his office. He added, his voice deepening, "I can't tell you how sorry I am to be doing this, Marcia."

"Yes," she said. "Is that all?"

He stood up, extending his hand across the desk. Reluctantly she took it; after Quentin's lean fingers, his hand felt pudgy and damp. She could think of absolutely nothing to say. Nodding at him, she turned on her heel and marched down the corridor, her face expressionless. Rosemary, thank goodness, was on her coffee-break. Not bothering to leave her a note, Marcia picked up her purse and left the building.

She got in her car and discovered that her knees were shaking. It took two tries to get the key in the ignition. She then headed for the Queensway, all her movements automatic, her brain as blank as her face. From the Queensway she took Route 17 east. The sun was shining and it was warm; she opened her window and let the wind blow through her hair. The traffic was fairly heavy. She wasn't the only person going east this sunny Friday afternoon. Probably many of the drivers were heading for their cottages along the river.

Cottage... *Quentin.*

She closed her mind against those two words, just as she had closed it against Dr. Martell's words, and drove steadily for two hours, leaving Ontario and entering Quebec, following the wide, lazy curve of the St. Lawrence River. Her gas gauge was getting dangerously low. She pulled in to a gas station, asked for a refill and went to the washroom. As she paid for the gas she picked up a bottle of ginger ale and a bag of chips, then took to the road again.

Behind her the sun sank lower in the sky. She'd had only a bowl of soup for lunch, and the chips and pop were pretty thin fare. At a quarter past six she stopped at a roadside restaurant that had several eighteen-wheelers parked outside; truckers always knew where the good meals were to be had.

The restaurant boasted vinyl-covered booths, rock music and a haze of blue smoke. Very different from where she'd eaten last night, thought Marcia, and as

though someone had physically punched her she felt the
words penetrate her consciousness. She looked at her
watch. Six-eighteen. Quentin would have expected her
home by now.

I can't phone him, she thought. I can't.

I've been fired. I've lost my job. I'm unemployed.

Acting on instinct alone, she went back to the phone
booth by the entrance, using her calling card and dialed
Lucy's number. Troy answered. She said rapidly, "Troy,
it's Marcia. Something's—something's happened and I
need a little time to myself. Will you phone Quentin and
tell him not to worry. I'll—"

"What's the matter?" he asked sharply.

"Tell him I'm all right. I'm just not sure when I'll be
back, so—"

"Marcia, you sound terrible. What's happened?"

"Please, Troy, will you do that for me? I just need to
be alone for a while, that's all... I've got to go, bye."
She crashed the receiver back on the hook and went back
into the restaurant. The volume of the music appeared
to have gone up by several notches. She ordered the roast
turkey dinner, choked it down, and followed it with two
cups of excellent coffee. She then went back to her car
and turned onto the highway, driving away from the
sunset.

Losing all track of time, Quentin had spent the day
sketching: strange, surreal sketches that were both an
abstraction and a mythicizing of what Marcia had called
his wallpapering efforts. At some deep level that pleased
him immensely. When the grandfather clock in the hall
chimed five, he dropped the stub of charcoal with an
exclamation of dismay and shoved back his chair. Marcia
would be home any minute.

He went into the kitchen and within fifteen minutes had reduced it to the kind of tidiness he knew she preferred. He then made the bed and gathered up the petals that had dropped from the flowers. He'd leave the papers on the wall for one more day.

He showered, cleaned up the bathroom and went back in the kitchen, opening a bottle of red wine and putting out some pâté and crackers. The better part of an hour had passed. She was late.

Although he picked up his sketchpad again, he couldn't concentrate, because subconsciously he was listening for the sound of her key turning in the lock and waiting to hear her voice. It was Friday, he thought. Today she'd promised to give him her answer. Whether she'd live with him. Or marry him.

Absently he poured himself a glass of wine and ate some pâté, going through the sketches one by one. With an inner certainty that had never yet failed him, he knew that they were good. What would Marcia think of them?

He wished she'd get home.

At six twenty-five the telephone rang in the kitchen. He ran for it and, not waiting for her to speak, said, "The wine's poured, the bed's made and all I need is you."

There was a small silence. Then a man's voice said noncommittally, "It's Troy speaking, Quentin. I just had a phone call from Marcia, and she asked me to get in touch with you."

Quentin's breath seemed to have lodged somewhere in the vicinity of his larynx. "Yes?" he croaked.

"She said something had happened and she needed some time alone. She's all right and you're not to worry."

"What the hell do you mean? *What's* happened? Where is she?"

"She wouldn't say."

His imagination running riot, Quentin rapped, "Maybe some guy had her at gunpoint."

"You're way off base, Quentin—Marcia would have found some way to let me know if that had been the case. This was something personal, I'd say."

"Where was she?"

"She didn't say and she rang off before I could ask. A public place of some kind—rock music, voices in the background—could have been a restaurant. A car pulled up while she was talking to me."

Quentin's frustration exploded in his voice. "That could be any bloody restaurant the width of the country."

Troy said carefully, "She did say you weren't to worry."

"Sorry," Quentin said. "Don't shoot the messenger, huh? But goddamn it, Troy, what's going on?"

"You've had a whirlwind romance—what's it been, three weeks? Maybe she just needs time to catch her breath."

"Then why call you and not me?"

"I don't know... She'll probably get in touch with you later," Troy said.

Her answer, Quentin thought. She didn't want to give him her answer because she knew he wouldn't like it. So she'd run away.

Her answer must be no.

Troy was saying something. Quentin fought to concentrate. "...in all evening if she calls again."

"You'll let me know if she does? I'm going to ring off, Troy, in case she's trying to reach me. Thanks."

He put down the phone and went back into the dining room. The sketches he'd been so proud of looked like messages from another country, meaningless scrawls not worth the paper they were drawn on. He drained his glass of wine and for the better part of an hour stayed where he was, willing the telephone to ring. Then he stood up, walking over to the window and staring out at the tidily arranged houses and the dull green waters of the canal.

He couldn't leave the condo in case Marcia phoned. Or came home. He was trapped in a square brick building in the middle of a city because he wanted a woman with hair like burnished wood and eyes the color of pansies. Wanted her more than he'd ever wanted anything in his life.

He'd lost his freedom.

What if he'd lost Marcia as well?

CHAPTER TWELVE

AT EIGHT-THIRTY that evening Marcia stopped at a small mall by the roadside and bought some toiletries, a nightgown and a change of clothes. At nine-thirty, exhausted, she booked a room in a motel, where she flicked on the television and sat mesmerized in front of the news channel for nearly an hour. One of the major oil companies was making layoffs. She buried her head in her hands and finally let the feelings that she'd been working so hard to repress wash over her.

She'd been fired. Her job was gone—the job that had been her life for seven years and the goal of her life all through university. Her job was her identity, she thought in terror. What would she be without it?

No one in her family had ever been fired. What would her great-grandfather, a thoracic surgeon, or her grandfather, a neurosurgeon, have thought of a member of the family who'd been ignominiously laid off?

Not much. And what of her clever, successful mother and her equally clever sister?

I'm ashamed of myself...I feel like a failure. The first tears slid down Marcia's cheeks. She cried for a long time, tears of anger and frustration and pain. Then she curled up in a ball on the bed and fell into a stunned sleep.

When she woke in the morning, she was reaching for Quentin. She had shared her bed with him for only two nights, and already she was used to him being there. Quentin wanted to marry her. But how could she marry him when she didn't have a job? Would she sponge off him? Put her hand out for money every time she needed anything? She couldn't do that. She wasn't cut out to be a kept woman. She was too independent.

Yesterday, she realized with an ugly lurch of her stomach, was the day she was to have given him her answer. On Thursday, in bed with him, she had wondered what might change between Thursday and Friday. She now knew. She couldn't possibly marry him. It wouldn't be fair to either one of them.

The pain she had felt last night was nothing to the pain she felt now, a pain that was beyond tears. With grim efficiency Marcia showered, breakfasted in the motel restaurant, and got back in her car. One thing had become clear to her in the night. She now knew where she was going. She was going to Holton, the little village in the Kennebecasis Valley in New Brunswick where Quentin had grown up.

She didn't know why yet, and rationally it made no sense at all. But it was her destination.

The miles rolled by, her little red car purring along smoothly. She reached the New Brunswick border, ate a late lunch at another truck stop, and by early evening had turned off the main highway into the valley. The river wound through open fields that merged into gentle wooded hills; red-winged blackbirds were singing in the reeds and bobolinks burbled above the tall grass of the meadows. There was an old-fashioned covered bridge over the river; she felt almost as though she were entering another century.

Holton consisted of a cluster of houses and a few farms, a post office, a gas station and a general store. Now that she was here, Marcia wasn't quite sure what she was going to do. She went into the general store and bought a chocolate bar, and said to the teenaged girl behind the counter, who was busily picking flakes of red polish from her fingernails, "Can you tell me where Quentin Ramsey used to live?"

"Never heard of him."

"I've come a long way," Marcia said. "Is there anyone else who could tell me?"

"I'll give Margie a call." She rolled her eyes. "Margie knows everyone in these parts."

After a lengthy conversation she put down the phone and said to Marcia, "Go right and follow the dirt road until you come to a yellow house. Ed and Kaye Miller. They'll tell you."

"Thanks," Marcia said, and hurried outside. Now that she was here, she was filled with a strange impatience. She soon found the yellow house. It was rundown, but there were big clumps of daffodils along the driveway and red-feathered hens pecking in the dirt by the porch. She took a deep breath and knocked on the front door.

It was flung open by a gangly old man with the most rambunctious eyebrows she'd ever seen. She said weakly, "I'm trying to find out where Quentin Ramsey used to live, Mr. Miller, and someone called Margie sent me here."

"You don't want to believe one word that comes out of that woman's mouth," he barked. "Worst gossip in fifty miles."

She took a step backward. "You can't help me, then?"

"Now, did I say that? Come along in—hurry up, else the house'll be singin' with mosquitoes, And call me Ed. Kaye!" he bellowed. "We got company... She's not feelin' that good—got a sore finger. I bin hollerin' at her all week to hike herself in to see the doctor, and does she listen? No, sirree."

He was tramping through a parlor complete with an upright organ and a horsehair sofa. Marcia followed him into the kitchen, which was clearly the hub of the house, with windows full of tall scarlet geraniums. Then footsteps shuffled into the room. Kaye Miller was wearing a print dress with a handknit cardigan; her hair was pure white, her eyes a gentle blue and her smile warm.

Marcia said quickly, "My name's Marcia Barnes. I'm from Ottawa, Mrs. Miller. I'm sorry to bother you, especially if you're not feeling well, but I was hoping to find out where Quentin Ramsey grew up, and I was directed here."

Kaye sat down in the rocking chair by the oil stove, nursing her right hand. Her face lit up with pleasure. "Well, now, how would you know Quentin?"

"We're—er—we're friends."

"Such a dear little boy, he was."

"Full of the old Nick," Ed growled.

"All boys are mischievous. And he's done so well for himself, painting those pictures."

"Them colors he uses—I wouldn't put 'em on a barn."

"Now, Edward," soothed Kaye. "What did you want to know, dear? Edward, why don't you put the teapot on?"

Amused to notice that Ed instantly headed for the stove, Marcia said, "I wondered if his parents were still alive, and where his house was."

"Ah, well...no, dear. His parents died when he was twelve. It was very sad, they drove off the road in a snowstorm. It changed him overnight; I do have to say that. Got real quiet, he did. The nearest relatives were in St. John, so he had to go and live in the city. Worst place in the world for a boy like him, who loved the outdoors so much."

"Ran wild from the time he was old enough to run," said Ed, getting three mugs from the cupboard and a can of milk from the refrigerator.

"The house had to be sold, of course—they left no money, not even for the funeral." Kaye sighed. "So the furniture went to auction and the Martins bought the house."

"Riffraff," Ed snorted.

"They weren't very nice people, certainly. The house burned to the ground a year later, so there was nowhere for Quentin to come back to—even if he'd been able to. We wanted to take him, but the uncle wouldn't hear of it."

Ed's opinion of the uncle was unrepeatable. "Now, Edward," said Kaye, and sighed again. "Not a good man, dear. We heard Quentin got in a lot of fights in the city. The townies always give the country boys a hard time. Broke his nose, and his wrist too, so we were told." She cheered up as Ed poured tea the color of coffee from the pot. "He always comes to visit us once a year, though. Such a lovely-looking man, isn't he?"

"Yes, he is," Marcia gulped, and blushed rosily.

The shame she'd felt over the loss of her job was nothing to the shame she felt now. She'd never even asked Quentin if his parents were alive; she hadn't asked about his broken nose or his childhood, or the village where he'd grown up. She'd been too absorbed in all the changes in her own life.

Selfish bitch, she thought venomously. How could she have been so mean-spirited, so self-centered?

So unloving.

Ed said testily, "You drove a long way to find this out. You plannin' on marryin' him?"

His question tapped into all her shame and confusion. But how could she evade those fiery old eyes. "He—he's asked me to."

"You could do a lot worse," said Ed.

"Now, Edward, you mustn't interfere. But why don't you get out some of the old albums? Perhaps Miss Barnes would like to see some photos of him when he was a boy."

"Please call me Marcia . . . and I'd love to."

But as Ed passed Kaye an old leather-bound album it slipped from his fingers and banged against her right hand; she gave a tiny shriek of pain. "What's the trouble?" Marcia asked in quick concern. "I'm a doctor—why don't you show me?"

The finger that Kaye showed her was puffy and inflamed. "That should be drained," Marcia said. "As soon as possible. I can't do it—I'm not a practising physician. Where's the nearest doctor?"

"Other side of the valley," Ed said promptly. "Ole Doc Meade—he'd take a look at it."

There had been no sign of a car outside the yellow house. "Why don't you check with him and I'll drive you there?" Marcia offered.

"Oh, we couldn't do that, dear."

"Friends of Quentin's are friends of mine," said Marcia, and knew that the simple words held a deeper meaning, one that was all-important to her.

One that she'd had to drive all this way to discover.

Since Troy's phone call on Friday evening, Quentin had passed the longest twenty-four hours of his life. The grandfather clock had ticked away the minutes and chimed the hours. His guts churning with an uncomfortable mixture of fury, desperation and anxiety, he had paced up and down, trying to eat a tuna sandwich that had tasted like sawdust and endeavoring not to drive himself crazy with worry.

His brain was a quagmire of questions, none of which he could answer. What in God's name had possessed

Marcia to run away? How could she have shared her bed
and her body and then simply disappeared without even
speaking to him? Was she afraid of him? Was that it?

These were not comforting thoughts. And as the time
passed with agonizing slowness the telephone had re-
mained deafeningly silent.

At two in the morning he had fallen asleep on the
chesterfield because he couldn't bear to use the bed. His
sleep had been riddled with nightmares that woke him
again and again to the harsh sounds of his own breathing
and to a loneliness blacker than any he had ever known.
Today had crept by at a snail's pace, until suddenly, at
four in the afternoon, he couldn't stand the silence and
solitude of his vigil any longer.

He'd gambled all his happiness on a woman he'd been
convinced was his soulmate, and he'd lost. He loved
Marcia with every fiber of his being. But she didn't love
him, and had lacked the courage to tell him so. The
sooner he faced up to that, the better.

Moving very slowly, Quentin began to gather his belongings. Picking up his clothes in the bedroom, he
flinched from the sight of the bed in which he had both
found and given—or so he'd thought—such felicity. He'd
been wrong there too, he thought dully. So much for
intuition. So much for his certainty that he'd found the
one woman who was his completion.

Although every movement felt as though he was
pushing his way through mud as thick as that on the
banks of the Kennebecasis, he persisted until there was
not a single mark left of his brief occupancy. Somehow,
during this activity, the patterns of years reasserted
themselves; he now knew exactly what he was
going to do.

He walked into the kitchen, looked up a number in the phone book, picked up the telephone and began to dial.

Marcia, Kaye and Ed left together for the doctor's. Ed was in the back seat, which in no way impeded his tongue. "Marcia, how come you ain't a proper doctor?" he demanded.

"I've been doing research ever since I graduated."

"Humph," said Ed. "Real people not good enough for you?"

Marcia remembered Jason falling from the step, and Quentin being so sick, and now Kaye's sore finger. On each occasion she'd said, I'm a doctor, and each time she'd been of use. I'm changing again, she thought in mingled excitement and panic. What's going on now?

"I got fired from my research job yesterday," she said, and somehow the words weren't difficult to say at all.

"Places in the backwoods, like Holton, they need a good doctor nearby. When ole Doc Meade passes on, Kaye an' me'll have to go into the city."

Quentin wanted to live in the country, so he could build her a house there. West coast or east, the country would have people like Ed and Kaye. "I haven't told Quentin I got fired."

Ed roared with uncouth laughter. "He got fired from every job he ever had. First sunny day, he'd take off to the woods. Bosses don't take kindly to that sort of thing."

"So you don't think it would matter to him?" she said blankly.

"Not likely!"

"I was ashamed to tell him. So I left town." Feeling as though a black pit had just opened in front of her, she gasped, "I ran away for nothing."

"You got that right," Ed remarked.

"Do you think he'll ever forgive me?"

"Of course he will, dear," Kaye said comfortingly.

"Tell you somethin' else," Ed put in. "I bet Quentin'd be a whole lot happier if you were a proper doctor—he was always lookin' after some scruffy ole raccoon, or an owl that one of the Martin kids had shot at. That research stuff—that's for people who ain't got the guts for real life."

Dr. Martell would not agree. But Marcia didn't work for Dr. Martell anymore. For the first time since she had gone into his office yesterday afternoon, she gained an inkling that it might be possible for her to view being fired as an opportunity for change rather than solely an occasion for shame.

"That's Doc Meade's place," Ed announced. "The next driveway."

Dr. Meade had his office in the basement of his house. Once Kaye and Ed were ushered in, Marcia sat quietly in a rickety wooden chair, going over all the events of the past two days in her mind. She now knew why she'd run away. The old Marcia had taken over—the woman who never shared her feelings with anyone. Especially the bad ones.

Quentin had threatened to leave her the last time she did that.

She looked around the room but there was no sign of a phone. I've got to talk to him, she thought frantically. I've got to tell him I made a terrible mistake and that I'm sorry.

Because I love him. I love him the way Lucy loves Troy. Good times and bad, for the rest of my life.

A beatific smile on her face, she sat very still. How could she have been so blind? So ignorant of her own feelings? Of course she loved Quentin. It had been staring her in the face for days.

As for Quentin, he wasn't in love with her salary or her position. He wasn't that kind of man. He was in love with her, the woman. A woman who might well become a country doctor. And if her change of career were to cause her great-grandfather and her grandfather to turn over in their respective graves, too bad. Lucy would approve. So would Troy. And so, she was certain, would Quentin.

She wanted to laugh and sing. She wanted to dance around the shabby little office between the worn wooden chairs. But most of all she wanted to tell Quentin she loved him. She wanted to hear his voice. To feel his arms around her.

It was a twelve-hour drive back to Ottawa.

In an agony of impatience she waited for Ed and Kaye. But when they came out they had Dr. Meade with them, a delightful old gentleman who didn't share Ed's low opinion of immunologists and wanted to hear all about her latest research. As briefly as good manners would allow, Marcia told him, then said craftily, "I should get Kaye home—it's been a long day for her. Nice to have met you, Dr. Meade. Goodbye."

As soon as they got home, Kaye sat down in the rocking chair and Ed put the kettle on again. Not sure if her digestive tract would survive more of his tea, Marcia said, "Do you mind if I use your phone? I have to talk to Quentin."

"Maybe we could have a word with him too, dear," Kaye said placidly. "We can tell him how kind you've been to us."

The telephone was attached to the kitchen wall. Marcia dialed her own number. It rang five times, then her answering machine clicked on. He's not home, she thought in despair, and said into the silence after the beep, "Quentin, I'm at Ed and Kaye's. I'll be back on Sunday. I love you. I'm *sorry* I ran away." She then replaced the receiver and tried the cottage. The phone rang and rang and no one picked it up.

Biting her lip, aware of Ed ostentatiously washing the mugs in the sink with a great clattering and splashing, she dialed Lucy and Troy's number. Troy answered. Marcia said in a rush, "Is Quentin there, Troy? It's Marcia."

"No, he's not," he said in a peculiar voice. "Where are you?"

"I'm in New Brunswick. In the village where Quentin grew up. Where is he, do you know? I've got to talk to him."

"You're too late," Troy said.

Her body went cold. *"Too late?"* she whispered.

"Sorry, sis, I didn't mean to scare you," Troy said hastily. "But he left two or three hours ago. He was going back to the cottage to get his gear, then he was catching a flight to Baffin Island."

"Baffin Island?" she repeated blankly.

"Yeah ... he has friends in Clyde River he thought he might visit."

"He didn't wait for me," Marcia said in a hollow voice.

"He wasn't in the mood to listen to reason. He'd figured out that you didn't want to marry him and that he'd pressured you too much, and he said he had to get the hell out of the city; it was driving him nuts sitting around waiting for you to come home when you obviously weren't going to. He was a tad angry that you'd run away too."

"I bet that's an understatement," said Marcia.

"We tried to talk to him... Well, you know Lucy, she didn't just talk, she lost her temper and yelled at him, but it didn't do any good. He left anyway."

"Oh, God," said Marcia. "I love him, you see. But I didn't know I did until tonight. And don't ask me to explain that because I can't. Do you know the names of his friends?"

"No. You could try paging him at the airport—I'll give you the number. It's the flight to Iqaluit... it might not have left."

"Thanks, Troy."

She dialed yet another set of digits, and when an official-sounding male voice answered she asked him to page Quentin Ramsey. "It's very important," she implored. "Please hurry."

But the slow minutes ticked by and Quentin didn't answer the call. When the official came back on she said numbly, "Thank you for trying. Goodbye," and leaned her forehead on the wall.

He'd gone. He'd left her because she hadn't had the guts to tell him she'd been fired.

He thought she didn't love him.

He thought her answer was no.

CHAPTER THIRTEEN

KAYE said tentatively, "Are you all right, Marcia?"

Remembering where she was, Marcia turned around. Kaye was watching her with concern and for once Ed was speechless. "Quentin's left," Marcia said. "He thinks I don't love him. So he's gone to Baffin Island. Baffin *Island*..." she finished in despair.

Ed snorted. "Kind of looks to me like he's got it all wrong. Or else you're a real good actress. You'd better hike yourself right after him."

Her jaw dropped. "Baffin Island's a big place."

"You'll find him," Ed said. "You don't even have to take vacation, 'cause you got fired."

Incredibly Marcia felt her mouth curve into the beginnings of a smile. "He has friends in Clyde River."

"Then you kin go there for starters. And you make sure when you find him you tell him right out that you love him—don't you go beatin' round the bush."

"You're right," said Marcia. "Am I a woman or a mouse? I really want that man, so I'd better make darn sure I do find him. There's not that many places in the Arctic, and he does tend to stand out in a crowd."

"You must stay the night," Kaye said pragmatically. "It wouldn't be safe for you to start out now. Ed's up before the rooster crows, so you can get away in good time in the morning."

So Marcia spent the evening looking through photo albums and listening to the two old people reminisce. Her heart ached at some of the shots of Quentin, a lanky boy with wiry black hair and laughing eyes, who'd lost parents and home and been consigned against his will to a city school with bullies who didn't like country boys. His intensity was the more easily understandable, as well as the darkness in so many of his paintings. No wonder he'd always been a nomad. No wonder he'd left Ottawa today to seek out the space and silence of the north.

Considering the amount of caffeine she'd drunk, she slept well, and by six-thirty the next morning she was ready to leave. "You make sure we get an invitation to the weddin'," Ed said.

"If there is one."

His brows positively bristled. "You cut out that 'if' stuff. I'll tell you, if I was younger I'd pound some sense into that fella myself—takin' off on a fine young woman like you. Kaye took a real shine to you—and she knows people, my Kaye does. And you make sure you stick to proper doctorin'."

"Yes, Ed," Marcia said meekly. Laughing up at him, she started her car. "I'll be in touch," she promised. As the hens scattered and the rooster charged down the slope in pursuit she drove onto the road and waved goodbye.

She didn't spend the whole day being as optimistic as Ed would have liked. The nearer she got to home the more she was convinced that Quentin wouldn't take her back, that she'd learned her lessons too late. She didn't cry, because she was possessed by a desperate urgency to get home, and she couldn't cry and drive at the same time. But her stomach was like a chunk of ice and her eyes burned and her hands were cold on the wheel. By the time she reached the outskirts of Ottawa, she felt sick with fear.

At the cloverleaf there was a sign for the airport. Without even thinking she followed it, turning off Route 17. She'd go there now and book a ticket on the first flight to Baffin Island. She didn't have the courage to

go back to her empty condo without the ticket in her
hand. Not when every room would be haunted with
memories.

But what if she went all the way to Clyde River and
Quentin didn't want her any more? What then?

At the airport Marcia parked her car and ran a comb
through her hair. She looked awful, she thought dis-
passionately. She was wearing the blouse she'd worn to
work on Friday along with the jeans and sweatshirt she'd
bought at the little mall; the sweatshirt was purple with
neon-tinted lupins drooping across her chest. The
shadows under her eyes were also purple.

The lupins reminded her of the flowers Quentin had
put in her bedroom. I won't cry, she told herself fiercely.
I will not.

She locked her car and walked to the terminal, her
legs protesting at the exercise. Her back ached. Her brain
was in overdrive. As for her emotions, in the last forty-
eight hours she'd surely made up for a lifetime of
suppression.

On her way to the ticket counter she passed the television screens that listed arrivals and departures. Her
eyes flicked over them. A flight had arrived from Iqaluit
twenty minutes ago. Like a woman in a dream she sought
out the signs for the baggage carousels and hurried
toward them, her face set. When she got to the baggage
area the crowd was thinning under the carousel labeled
with the Iqaluit flight number, and not one of the pas-
sengers was Quentin.

Through a crushing disappointment she scolded herself
for being such a fool. Quentin had only just gone there.
Why would he turn around and come straight back?

Especially if he didn't love her any more.

It was a good thing Ed wasn't here, Marcia thought,
holding tight to the remnants of her composure; Ed

would have given her merry old hell for thinking so negatively.

She turned on her heel to go back to the ticket area, and as though her need had conjured him up she saw the man standing in front of one of the telephones on the far wall. Although his back was to her, she would have known him anywhere. He had just dialed a number and was waiting for the connection, the cold fluorescent lighting falling on his untidy black curls. He was wearing a dark blue sweater and jeans, hiking boots on his feet. Her heart crowding its way into her throat, she stood frozen to the floor.

He slammed the receiver down and ran his fingers through his hair. Then he slung the duffel bag that had been at his feet over one shoulder and headed for the exit. He looked in worse shape than she was.

He hadn't seen her. "Quentin!" Marcia shouted in a cracked voice. "Quentin!" And as if it were happening in slow motion she saw his head turn. Paralyzed by a storm of emotions, the uppermost of which was terror, she found herself quite unable to move, her feet like lumps of lead. Their eyes met, and for a moment that seemed to last forever he stood as still as she. Then he started toward her, his face unreadable.

He loves me, he loves me not, she thought idiotically, and watched him come to a halt two feet away from her. Letting his bag slide to the floor, he said in a level voice, "I just tried to phone you."

"I'm not home."

The ghost of a smile crossed his face; his eyes were deepset, bruised with fatigue, and his jaw stubbled with a dark beard. "I see that, Marcia. What are you doing here?"

"I came to the airport to buy a ticket for Clyde River. I don't even know where Clyde River is."

"East coast of Baffin Island," he said, his features carefully blank. "Why were you going there?"

"You're not making this any easier," she complained. "And you look even worse than I do."

"I've just been through the worst two days of my entire life, and I've had a few bad ones to compare it with. You don't look so hot yourself. You should give that sweatshirt away—not that anyone would take it."

"I'd better hold onto it," she said, "considering I lost my job on Friday."

Something flared in his eyes and was gone. "Did you, now? For being late three days in a row?"

"No, Quentin. Government cutbacks."

"So did you hide at the institute for the weekend? Where, of course, all the telephones were out of order?"

She had known he was angry, but not quite this angry. "I spent last night with Ed and Kaye," she said roundly.

Surprise, fury and relief followed each other across his face. "Now what did you do that for?" he asked with spurious calm.

She blurted, "Quentin, do you still love me?"

"Do you think I flew to Iqaluit and back in the space of twenty-four hours for fun?" he exploded. "Of course I still love you. I'm stuck with loving you for the rest of my goddamned life."

He did not look happy at this prospect. "Oh," Marcia said in a small voice, her heart beginning to sing in her breast, "that's good. Because I love you too."

"Listen to me, Marcia Barnes—I'm dirty, unshaven, hungry, thirsty and exhausted. Don't play games with me—I'm not in the mood!"

"I'm not playing games," she retorted, and repeated in less than lover-like tones, "I love you—I finally figured it out." In an effort to get rid of the crippling tension in her chest, she raised her voice over the whining of the carousels and the clatter of baggage carts. "I love you, Quentin Ramsey! I love you right now, I'll love you tomorrow and all next week, and I suspect that I, too, am stuck with loving you for the rest of my life. Goddamned or otherwise."

There was a smattering of laughter from some passersby. Quentin looked around, baring his teeth in a raffish grin. "Let's see if you'll put your money where your mouth is. Will you marry me?"

She said pertly, "Would you marry me in this sweatshirt?"

"God help me, I would."

"Okay," she said.

The line of his jaw relaxed a little. But he had yet to touch her. He said abruptly, "This is all very amusing, but I hate airports. Let's go home."

"Where is home? I don't even know that any more."

"I don't think either one of us is capable of driving to the cottage right now. Your place?"

She nodded. "My car's outside."

"So's mine. Let's go."

Marcia stood her ground, her heart thumping underneath the lupins. "Quentin, kiss me."

He took her by the shoulders, planted a passionate and passionately angry kiss on her lips and stood back, his chest heaving. Then he hoisted his bag over his shoulder and started for the door.

Marcia followed, trotting along behind like an obedient wife. His beard had scraped her chin, and unless she was mistaken they were headed for the biggest fight of their not particularly placid courtship. All right, she thought, if that's the way you want to play it, I'll be glad to oblige, and said coldly, after they had crossed to the car park, "My car's over there. I'll see you in a few minutes."

He gave her a curt nod and strode off between the closely packed rows of cars. Twenty minutes later, when Marcia took the elevator to her floor, Quentin was already unlocking her door. His gaze far from friendly, he said, "Who's first for the shower?"

"You shave and I'll shower, then I'll dry my hair while you shower," she said, and walked inside. "You took the drawings down!"

"I burned them. At the cottage."

She stalked down the hall to her bedroom, not surprised to find it bare of floral offerings. The whole place looked bare; he'd removed every trace of his stay. She grabbed a very unsexy cotton nightgown from her drawer along with an old terry robe she'd had for at least six years and headed for the bathroom. Stripping off her clothes, not caring if he was watching her or not, she stepped into the shower.

The stingingly hot water diluted her temper and relaxed her muscles. She wrapped her body in one towel and her hair in another, and stepped out onto the mat. Quentin was bent over the sink, rinsing his chin; he was naked, his back curved like a bow, his long legs arrowstraight. She fled to her bedroom and dried her hair in front of the mirror. Belting her robe tightly round her waist, she then went into the kitchen.

She hadn't eaten for what felt like a very long time. And Quentin had mentioned hunger among his list of woes. She banged a saucepan on the stove with unnecessary force and heard him say, "What are you making?"

"Oatmeal with raisins, brown sugar and cream," she announced. He was wearing his jeans slung low on his hips and nothing else; her eyes skidded away. "Comfort food. What did you do with all my flowers?"

"I trashed them," he said. "I'll make myself a tuna sandwich. My aunt made oatmeal three hundred and sixty-five days a year and I haven't touched it since."

Her fingernails were digging into the rim of the saucepan. "How old were you when you left them, Quentin—your aunt and uncle, I mean?"

"Sixteen. Minimum legal age."

She had known the answer before she asked the question. "I love you," she said helplessly. "I love you, and we're behaving like a couple of stray cats."

He walked up to her, detached her fingers from the saucepan and held them captive in his own, his blue eyes piercing through all her defenses, his voice harsh. "Why didn't you tell me you lost your job? Why did you run away?"

At some level Marcia had known this was the question he would ask, to which he deserved the most honest answer she could give. She rested her free hand on top of his and let him see all her bewilderment and pain. "There'd been rumors flying all week, but I never really believed they'd affect me. Then on Friday at two o'clock I was told I was out of a job. Just like that.

"I come from a family of achievers, Quentin—physicians back four generations—and I'm the first one ever to be fired. I felt humiliated and ashamed, as though I wasn't worth anything. It was also quite clear to me that I'm not cut out to go asking you for money—I'm too used to being independent. So—"

"I don't give a damn if you've got a fortune stashed under the mattress or if you're penniless! That's never been an issue. It's *you* I love. Not your money or your career."

"I was too upset on Friday to realize that."

"You could have asked," he said with dangerous softness. "You could have told me what was going on."

"I'm *sorry*. I didn't even think—I just ran."

"And phoned Troy instead of me. How do you think that made me feel?"

"I was too humiliated to talk to you!"

"Do you know what I thought had happened?" he said, his voice rising. "I thought your answer was no—you didn't want to live with me or marry me. And you'd lacked the courage—or the common courtesy—to tell me face to face, so you'd run away. That's why I stripped this place bare of every mark I'd made on it, and that's why I headed north. I'd misjudged you ever since I'd met you. That's what I thought."

Briefly she closed her eyes. "I'm more sorry than I can say. But for the space of twenty-four hours I felt as though I'd lost my identity, as though I didn't know who I was any more... It took Ed Miller to knock some sense into me. I don't know why I headed east on Friday afternoon; it wasn't a conscious decision. But don't you see, Quentin? Even while I was running away from you I was running toward you too."

He let out his breath in a long sigh, the muscles rippling across his bare chest. "Yeah..." he said. "I only wish I'd known what was going on."

"I wish I'd had the courage—or the smarts—to tell you," she said stonily.

He brought her hand to his mouth, pressing his lips into the hollow at her wrist where the veins showed blue and her pulse bumped against her skin. "So you went straight to Holton?"

She nodded. "I've never asked you about your childhood, have I? Or what happened to your parents. I felt ashamed of myself for that too. But from Ed and Kaye I found out why you've always been a nomad and how much you must love me to have stuck it out with me in a condo in the city." With passionate intensity she added, "I'll do my best never to take away your freedom, Quentin."

His heart was thudding in his chest. "You traveled a long way," he said obliquely. "If I was less than friendly at the airport it was because I discovered when I got to Iqaluit that freedom for me now means being with you. I couldn't stay there. I had to come back. But all along I'd given you the very best gifts of my body and my talent and my heart, and they hadn't been enough—you'd run away. When I saw you at the airport, I was so strung out I figured I was hallucinating."

"Oh, no," said Marcia. "I'm real." Raising his hand to her cheek, she added, "Ed suggested—and I think he's right—that I should become a real doctor. A proper doctor. Like ole Doc Meade."

"Is he still around?" Quentin threw back his head and laughed. "The day I had the brush with the porcupine, he picked quills out of my knee for a solid hour. You'd make a great Doc Meade, Marcia."

"I might have to go back to university for a year."

"That'll give me time to build our house."

"You really do want to marry me?"

His arms found their way around her waist. "Yes," he said.

A sheen of tears in her eyes, she confessed, "By the time I'd reached the Quebec border, I'd convinced myself you didn't love me any more. Quentin, I won't ever run away again—I swear." Her brow furrowed in thought. "I don't know why I had to go to Holton to find out that I love you. But now that I know I do—why, that makes you my safe haven, doesn't it? The one person I can tell anything to... Am I making any sense?"

He said succinctly, "You learned a lot at Kaye and Ed's."

"Ed wants an invitation to the wedding."

"I wouldn't think of getting married without him."
Quentin pulled her closer and kissed her with lingering
sensuality. "Dearest and most adorable Marcia, I love
you. I suspect our marriage will never be dull and tomorrow morning I'm going to buy you a housecoat that's
just the tiniest bit sexier than the one you're wearing.
And some more flowers." He moved his hips against
hers. "But right now you have a choice to make. Oatmeal
or me."

Fluttering her lashes and linking her hands behind his
neck, she said, "Are you saying you prefer me to a tunafish sandwich?"

"I think that's what I'm trying to get across."

Desire flooded her, hot and compelling. "You're succeeding," she said. "You're very definitely succeeding.
I can always have oatmeal for breakfast."

Unbelting her robe, he caressed the soft swell of her
breasts. "Someday soon I'll ravish you against the
stove," he said. "But not tonight. Tonight I think we
both need to be in bed."

So they went to bed and made love. They then got up
and made tunafish sandwiches and oatmeal. They
phoned Lucy and Evelyn and Cat and Ed and announced their engagement. They went back to bed and
made love again.

And two months later, when they'd come back from
their honeymoon in New Brunswick and were packing
all their belongings in a moving van to go out west—
where Marcia was to do a residency in family medicine
and Quentin was to build a house—there were three
paintings in crates in the van: the woman in the red dress,
the three little girls running through a field and a big
canvas covered with spirals of vibrant color—the canvas
that had been Marcia's first introduction to the
man she loved.

HARLEQUIN PRESENTS°

Read the first story in Robyn Donald's intriguing new trilogy:

THE MARRIAGE MAKER

Olivia Nicholls and half sisters Anet and Jan Currethers
are all linked by a mysterious portrait that is meant to
bring love to the lives of those who possess it—but
there is one condition....

This is Olivia's story:

#1865 THE MIRROR BRIDE

Available in February wherever
Harlequin books are sold.

Take 4 bestselling love stories FREE

Plus get a FREE surprise gift!

Special Limited-time Offer

Mail to Harlequin Reader Service®

3010 Walden Avenue
P.O. Box 1867
Buffalo, N.Y. 14240-1867

YES! Please send me 4 free Harlequin Presents® novels and my free surprise gift. Then send me 6 brand-new novels every month, which I will receive months before they appear in bookstores. Bill me at the low price of $2.90 each plus 25¢ delivery and applicable sales tax, if any*. That's the complete price and a savings of over 10% off the cover prices—quite a bargain! I understand that accepting the books and gift places me under no obligation ever to buy any books. I can always return a shipment and cancel at any time. Even if I never buy another book from Harlequin, the 4 free books and the surprise gift are mine to keep forever.

106 BPA A3UL

Name	(PLEASE PRINT)	
Address		Apt. No.
City	State	Zip

This offer is limited to one order per household and not valid to present Harlequin Presents® subscribers. *Terms and prices are subject to change without notice. Sales tax applicable in N.Y.

UPRES-696

©1990 Harlequin Enterprises Limited

HARLEQUIN PRESENTS®

A new story from one of Harlequin Presents' most
popular authors

#1863 ONE-MAN WOMAN
by
Carole Mortimer

Ellie was only interested in one-to-one relationships,
so Daniel Thackery wasn't for her. But she had
to keep him talking: he seemed to be up to no
good and—even more important—he knew the
whereabouts of her sister's estranged husband.
Only Ellie's persistence seemed to encourage
Daniel to think that she could yet
become his woman!

Available in February wherever
Harlequin books are sold.

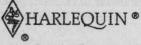

Harlequin and Silhouette celebrate
Black History Month with seven terrific titles,
featuring the all-new *Fever Rising*
by Maggie Ferguson
(Harlequin Intrigue #408) and
A Family Wedding by Angela Benson
(Silhouette Special Edition #1085)!

Also available are:
Looks Are Deceiving by Maggie Ferguson
Crime of Passion by Maggie Ferguson
Adam and Eva by Sandra Kitt
Unforgivable by Joyce McGill
Blood Sympathy by Reginald Hill

On sale in January at your favorite
Harlequin and Silhouette retail outlet.

HARLEQUIN ® Silhouette®

You're About to Become a

Privileged Woman

Reap the rewards of fabulous free gifts and benefits with proofs-of-purchase from Harlequin and Silhouette books

Pages & Privileges™

It's our way of thanking you for buying our books at your favorite retail stores.

Harlequin and Silhouette—
the most privileged readers in the world!

For more information about Harlequin and Silhouette's PAGES & PRIVILEGES program call the Pages & Privileges Benefits Desk: 1-503-794-2499

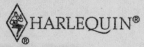

HARLEQUIN®